QUIET PLACES

JASPER BARK

Let the world know:
#IGotMyCLPBook!

Crystal Lake Publishing
www.CrystalLakePub.com

WELCOME
TO ANOTHER

CRYSTAL LAKE PUBLISHING
CREATION

For
Lady Fiona Hannon,
a fine Highland lass, much missed by her son-in-law
and her family.
And
Sheana Bark
who has a touch of the Highlands and is much loved
by her son.

WELCOME TO DUNBALLAN, GENTLE READER, AND WELCOME TO ANOTHER TITLE IN THE BARK BITES HORROR LINE.
DUNBALLAN IS A TINY HIGHLANDS TOWN THAT'S YET TO JOIN THE 21ST CENTURY, ALL THE BETTER TO KEEP ITS DARK SECRETS. AND TO KEEP DAVID CAVENDISH IN ITS DARK GRIP.
ONLY HIS LOVER, SALLY CAN PRY HIM LOOSE, BUT TO DO SO SHE MAY HAVE TO ALLY HERSELF WITH FORCES DARKER THAN ANYTHING THAT HOLDS DAVID IN ITS THRALL AND IN THE PROCESS SHE MAY JUST LEARN THAT THE QUIET PLACES ARE OFTEN THE MOST TERRIFYING.
POLIWKO

PROLOGUE

THEY WERE WAITING for her on Dundooan Road.

Sally turned the corner and there they were—an older woman and a young boy, who looked very much alike. They were obviously mother and son. Neither of them noticed Sally, they simply stared straight ahead with glazed eyes.

The mother was short and thickset, wearing a woollen hat, a long raincoat and carrying an old cloth shopping bag. The son was about twelve years old, skinny and pale with black hair. He wore a hoodie, jeans and trainers.

There was no expression on their faces, their jaws were slack and their mouths hung open. The son was standing a few steps behind his mother, his right arm swung backwards and forwards in a shallow arc. The mother was swaying slightly, as if the shopping bag was about to overbalance her. There was nothing going on behind their eyes, no mental faculties of any sort. They were completely soulless, everyone in Dunballan was. Everyone except for Sally.

She walked over to the mother and son to get a closer look at them. The mother's breathing was irregular and sounded like dried peas rattling in a box. Her eyes were cloudy and opalescent, so were the son's. Sally hadn't seen that before.

They must have been outside on the night it happened, the night Sally hated to think about, when everyone in Dunballan changed. Most people had been in doors when it occurred, but Sally occasionally came across a few unlucky ones who were caught in the street.

Dundooan Road was on the outskirts of Dunballan, so she'd only just gotten to it. This meant the mother and son had been out in the open for nearly eight days and were suffering the effects of exposure and dehydration. The first thing Sally had to do was get them in doors.

"Come on you," Sally said. She put her hands on the mother's shoulder and began to turn her. The people she found in this condition were usually very compliant and though they didn't have any consciousness, they would walk or move wherever Sally guided them.

The mother was ice cold, like a corpse. She might not live much longer. She began to turn, took one step, faltered and pitched forward colliding with Sally. She was much heavier than she looked. Sally's legs went from under her and she fell onto her back. The mother crashed down on top of her.

A sharp pain shot through Sally's shoulder blades as she hit the pavement and the breath was knocked out of her. The mother's forehead smashed into Sally's cheek, making her wince and cry out. She could smell the woman's breath, sour and rank like rotted flesh. It rattled in her throat as she took one last painful breath, shuddered and went limp.

As the mother's muscles relaxed and lost all their tension, her body became heavier, pinning Sally to the ground. Sally tried to push her off, but she was too limp, too much of a dead weight to move. She was crushing Sally's chest, and Sally found it hard to catch her breath.

"Get off me," she shouted at the corpse, as though that would help. She didn't want to be trapped outside with a dead woman on top of her. She'd hardly slept, hardly eaten, and she didn't have the energy to shove it off.

Sally's only hope was to wriggle out from underneath the dead mother. So, she rocked herself backwards and forwards, scraping her elbows and her backside, but managed to get her left arm and leg out from under the corpse. This gave her enough purchase to use the weight of the body to her benefit, pushing against it with her left arm while she pulled her right arm free and manoeuvred her right leg out from under it.

Sally got to her feet, sore and out of breath, and walked over to the boy. He hadn't moved or changed his position one bit. He was still staring straight ahead and swinging his arm. She touched his cheek and unlike his stone cold mother, he seemed to have a temperature. He probably wouldn't last much longer himself, but she still had to get him inside. She would deal with the mother's corpse later, when she had time.

"Come with me," she said and took hold of the boy's hand. He didn't show any signs that he'd heard her, or even knew she was there, but he walked after her without any resistance. Sally led him to the door of the nearest cottage. As she reached for the handle, she felt something brush the back of her leg.

She looked behind her and saw a small black cat at her feet. Its fur was matted and its bones were beginning to show under its coat, but Sally couldn't help but feel a tiny moment of excitement. Could the cat have wandered in from outside Dunballan? Might there be one other fully conscious being here apart from her?

She bent down and picked up the cat, stroking it as she lifted it up and looked into its eyes. It went limp in her hands, all the life drained from its muscles. It had no more awareness than the mother or her son. Neither did it have a soul.

Sally scolded herself for getting her hopes up. There wasn't a single living thing in Dunballan with a soul, even the birds and the animals were affected. Sally knew that she was just being foolish. She put the cat back on the ground. It swayed but remained on its feet, then carried on along the cracked paving stones, moving from pure muscle memory. In a few days it would probably be dead.

Sally felt a huge pang of guilt about all the pets and other animals she was allowing to starve. She just didn't have time to feed them all and most didn't eat even when she put food down for them. They just stared straight ahead, panting, but showing no other signs of life.

Sally tried the door of the cottage and was surprised to find it was locked. This was unusual for Dunballan. It was a remote town and people from outside hardly ever visited, everyone knew their neighbours' business and, as a consequence, very few people locked their doors.

Sally examined the front door, which had a single

Yale lock but no mortise. She'd learned a lot about locks in the last eight days, especially how to break into the few that were locked. The Yale lock was over twenty years old, so opening it wasn't an issue.

She reached into her pocket and pulled out a credit card. She worked the card between the frame and the door, and then slid it into the lock mechanism and released the latch.

The door swung open and a familiar stench wafted out from the hallway. It was in every house she entered—unwashed bodies, stale air and human waste. A sad, pitiable smell that Sally would never get used to, a constant reminder of how desperate things had become.

Sally led the boy down the hall and opened the first door on her left, which led into the living room. There was one other person in the room—a short, thin lady in her mid-fifties sitting in an armchair, gazing into space, her jaw hanging slack. The roots were showing in her dyed brunette hair and there were flakes of dandruff on the shoulders of her cardigan. She didn't pay Sally any attention. Her only movements were the rise and fall of her chest and the occasional slow blink.

The boy allowed himself to be brought into the room and Sally got him to lie down, on the sofa, and then she covered him with a blanket she found. He offered no resistance. His cloudy eyes simply gazed into the distance at nothing at all. He was burning up. Sally needed to find more blankets and get some water into him.

The television was still on, tuned to a shopping channel. The presenter was extolling the virtues of incontinence pants. Sally looked at the yellow and brown stains that spilled out from underneath the woman and thought this ironic. The woman had been in the same position for the last eight days, but her bowels hadn't stopped working. Sally would clean her up, as soon as she'd tended to the boy, but she wasn't looking forward to it.

She found the kitchen at the back of the house. A tall man, with broad shoulders and wavy ginger hair, greying at the temples, stood at the counter next to the sink. He seemed familiar to Sally, but she wasn't sure where she'd seen him before.

He was staring at the wall in front of him, rocking gently from foot to foot. He paid no attention to her, his eyes were glassy and his expression vacant. He was holding his left hand out in front of him, the fingers bunched into a fist. It looked like there was something in them.

On the counter in front of him were mugs, a packet of tea bags and a bottle of rancid milk. He must have been making a cuppa when it hit, and he hadn't left that position since. There was a large wet stain around the crotch of his grey flannel trousers and a big brown lump bulged at the back. Some of it had spilled over the top of his waistband and stained his shirt. Another loose pile had found its way down his trouser leg and onto the floor. His heel caught it every time he rocked, making a tiny squelch.

Sally wrinkled her nose. She took one of the mugs from the counter, blew the dust out of it and filled it with water from the sink. She held the mug up to the man's cracked lips, and he swallowed the water automatically without showing any other sign of consciousness. Sally was aware that she should be helping the boy first, but she was here in the kitchen and the boy might not last much longer. The man had a better chance of survival.

She decided to check the cupboards to see if there were any tins, or packets of soup she could heat to feed them. Soup was the best thing because they were less likely to choke on it. She didn't find any tins or packets, so she checked the fridge. It was full of raw meat that was starting to spoil. Sally would have to check for soup in the neighbouring houses and come back to feed them later.

She pulled a chair out from the kitchen table and sat down. A wave of exhaustion washed over at the thought of traipsing backwards and forwards between houses with soup. She was so tired she could feel it in her bones. She cradled her head in her hands and sobbed with exhaustion.

She'd visited fourteen houses already today, and she'd hardly had anything to eat herself. She hadn't slept more than two or three hours a night in over a week. She wasn't certain how much longer she could keep this up. Every living creature in Dunballan needed her care, they were all empty vessels left idling. If Sally didn't look after them, they would keel over and die like the mother in the street.

Fairly soon she would have to start making difficult decisions about who lived and who didn't. Dunballan was a small town, but there were still over two thousand people living there, if you could call what they did living. Sally couldn't feed all of them, or clean up after each of them, there simply wasn't time, and she didn't have the physical energy to care for them all. Her life was already one long round of drudgery, breaking into their homes, searching their larders for food.

Then there were the bodies she had to pull from crashed cars, and the corpses that had fallen from ladders, or scaffolding. They had to be disposed of and there was never enough time to do that, not if she wanted to keep all the others alive.

As the wave of despondency and helplessness threatened to overwhelm her, she felt new emotions growing in her chest—guilt and recrimination. It was a familiar cycle, one she went through at least once a day. This was her job, nobody else could deal with this. She couldn't get the authorities in, they wouldn't believe her if she told them what had really happened.

This was her burden and hers alone. She had to step up and cope with the aftermath as best she could.

Sally got to her feet, trying to ignore the knot of pain between her shoulder blades and the bruises she got from the fall. She went back to the sink to get some water for the boy. As she was running the water, the man caught her eye again. She was curious about what he held in his left hand. She reached over to him and tried to open his hand, but the man resisted her. This wasn't normal. They usually did whatever she told them to.

His hand was rough and calloused but surprisingly warm. Touching it brought back a sudden memory and she knew exactly who he was, or who he'd once been. He was the local butcher. Sally had been in his shop only eight days ago, when Dunballan had been an entirely different place.

If Sally hadn't gone into his shop, if she hadn't carried out her mad escapade, then nothing would be like it was now.

CHAPTER 1

THE BUTCHER SHOP'S door had an old fashioned bell, which rang every time a customer entered. The butcher looked up as Sally came in, and greeted her with a warm smile that had a worrying proprietary edge. Sally avoided his light brown eyes, but couldn't help noticing the freckles on his nose and his thick wet lips.

"And what can I be doing for you?" he asked, modifying his brogue, because Sally was an off-comer.

"I'd like some steak," Sally said. "The best you have."

The butcher's smile broadened.

"Romance is in the air tonight," he said. "It's the big man's lucky night, is it?" Sally demurred and looked down at the black and white tiles of the floor. "As it happens you're in luck," he said. "I have a nice piece of dry hung tenderloin for you. How thick would you like it cut?"

"An inch or so, I guess."

"An inch and a half is best, keeps it nice and tender on the inside, just like me," he said with a wink.

"Okay."

"And how many will you be wanting?"

"Eight."

The butcher raised his eyebrows. "Eight?"

"No, ten."

"Are you having company? Visitors to the town perhaps? We don't get many of those."

Sally ignored the question. The smile fell from the Butcher's face, and he went to cut the meat.

The smile was back as he laid the cuts on the counter.

"Just look at that marbling," he said, pointing out the thick veins of fat. "Best to grill these, make sure the pan's nice and hot mind. Couple of minutes each side and cover them with butter before you do, clarified is best. Don't forget the salt and pepper either, rub it in beforehand, use those soft little fingers of yours." He smiled again, but it teetered on the brink of becoming a leer.

Sally chose not to respond.

The butcher wrapped the steaks carefully and popped them in a large plastic bag. His fingers stroked Sally's as he handed the bag over. "This'll put lead in his pencil, I can promise you that."

Sally flushed in spite of herself, hating the way her cheeks burned as she paid for the meat. How dare he touch her like that? She turned and left the shop without saying another word.

The meat was a cold, heavy lump in her bag as she strode up the tiny high street. She ground her teeth and breathed heavily through her nose, burning with anger at the butcher's presumption and insinuations.

Sally got to the corner of the high street and looked up for the first time as she crossed the cobblestone road. She passed three middle aged housewives who'd gathered on the opposite corner, trying not to catch their eyes. They stopped their conversation mid-sentence and turned to watch her.

They smiled at Sally as she went by and on each of their faces she saw the same proprietorial look the butcher had. She turned away from them with her chin in the air. She wasn't going to give them the satisfaction.

She knew they were aware of what was happening to her and David, and she knew they approved, the whole town did. It was there behind their eyes and their expectant smiles, every time she met them. They needed her to go through what she was going through, for reasons they would never divulge.

She'd mentioned this to David when they first moved to Dunballan. She'd tried to make light of it, turn it into a shared joke, but David had closed down on her as he so often did. When she tried to push him, he told her she just wasn't used to living in a small town. Most of the town's families had lived there for centuries, and they didn't get many off-comers.

David's ancestors, the McCavendish clan, had once been Lairds of the manor. Their estates had been sold off long ago, but they were still seen as the town's first family, and David was the sole surviving heir.

His arrival had been greeted as a big occasion by the townsfolk. Sally had thought it quaint, at first, when the older folk doffed their caps to David. After a while, it simply added to the claustrophobia she felt. She and David were under constant scrutiny. The townsfolk radiated a perpetual sense of expectation, and Sally felt herself slowly crushed by its weight.

As she got to the outskirts of town, Sally's mood calmed, her anger subsided and her sense of purpose returned. She reached the shortcut that she always used on her way home, a cut between two terraced houses, with an arched stone entrance that gave out onto a steep set of steps.

The stone steps were cut into the hillside, bordered on either side by hedgerows, a single wooden railing running alongside them. As she was about halfway up the steps, a sudden wind shook the hedges, dry leaves skittered on the ground and the branches rustled in the hedgerow. Sally stopped and tilted her head, listening for any signs of a presence in the undergrowth, or an inkling of a voice.

Footsteps clattered on the steps below. "Sally!" a voice called out. Sally took a deep breath. She thought she'd gotten away. She didn't bother to hide her irritation as she turned and saw Jane, the town librarian, huffing up the steps.

"Sally, I . . . oh goodness . . . just let me get my breath a moment," Jane said, resting a hand on the frail wooden railing. She was a tall woman, with brown, bobbed hair that framed her pinched face like a pair of old theatre curtains. She was probably in her late thirties, but she was dressed like an old maid, in a tweed skirt and a hand knitted cardigan.

"I'm sorry," she said. "I saw you coming up the steps and I ran after you." Jane paused for a moment, waiting for Sally to say something, but she didn't. Jane ran a hand through her hair and took a deep breath. "Did you err . . . did you read the pamphlet I gave you?"

"Yes."

"Well that's what I . . . what I wanted to talk to you about." There was another pause. Sally didn't know what Jane expected her to say. Probably something about the pamphlet, a thick volume on local folklore.

"I thought you had a right to know," Jane said. "That's why I gave it to you. But I wouldn't want you . . . that is, I don't think you should do anything rash." Jane took a breath, weighing her words. "The people of this town, they're not . . . we're not bad people. I thought you should know there's a reason for everything that's happening, that's all. That's why I gave you the pamphlet. I . . . well, I don't want to be presumptuous, but I thought it might help. I . . . I thought you should know."

She looked up at Sally from the lower step and her face was lit with a timid hope. She still wanted to connect with Sally. She knew what Sally was going through, just like the rest of the town, yet she still had the temerity to think they could be friends. She'd given Sally the pamphlet, practically rubbing her face in it and now she wanted Sally to be all understanding. Sally could have slapped her stupid face.

Sally couldn't go back to the library, not after what she'd learned, no matter how much she loved to read. Books weren't just an escape from her daily life in Dunballan, they were about the only contact she had with the outside world.

There was no phone coverage anywhere in the town, and the remote cottage where she lived with David didn't even have a landline. You had to drive five miles up the road before you got any signal, and there was no broadband either. Sally hadn't believed it when they first moved in, but after several hours of shouting at company reps from a pay-phone, she found that not only did no one want it, they'd campaigned against laying any cables.

The town's only newsagent carried nothing but the local paper, the Sunday Post and ageing copies of The People's Friend. Dunballan clung doggedly to its remoteness and refused to join the twenty-first century. The only light in this tunnel of seclusion had been the town library which was surprisingly well-stocked with a good selection of modern books.

Jane had remarkably similar taste to Sally and had begun recommending books and authors to her. Jane's recommendations were excellent, but her attempts to engage Sally in conversation were stilted and self-conscious, often leaving Sally feeling awkward and embarrassed. There are some people with whom, in spite of the best intentions, you just never click. Jane was one of them.

Sally knew Jane was reaching out to her. She knew Jane wanted to be friends, and heaven knows she needed one, but not Jane. The longer they failed to connect, the more strained their relations became.

Finally Jane had given her the little pamphlet on folklore, it was her last attempt to forge a friendship. It hadn't worked. The pamphlet had just infuriated Sally. It had shown her how complicit everyone in the town was in her suffering, and she could never forgive them, least of all Jane.

Now she stood staring earnestly up at Sally like some expectant suitor, and Sally could have throttled her, picked up a brick and bashed her earnest face in.

The flies from the hedgerow had begun to notice the meat in Sally's bag. She waved them away and pulled the top of the bag shut.

"Okay," was all Sally said, even that was hard to get out. She turned her back and continued up the steps.

CHAPTER 2

SALLY OPENED HER back gate and stepped into the garden. She glanced at all the unplanted rows she and David had dug when they planned to make an allotment.

The beans she'd planted had begun to sprout. The warm weather was good for them. The little row of canes was half-finished, and the rest of the trench was empty. Sally was sorry now that they hadn't completed it. Like so many things in their relationship, it was left unfinished.

A sudden wind sprang up from the west. It bent the trees in the fields next to the cottage, but it was neither hot nor cold. It ruffled the grass, rattled the hedges, and lifted Sally's hair and skirt, but she couldn't feel it on her skin, nor could she smell any of the scents that a wind such as this usually carried. It was almost entirely bodiless, you could see and experience its effects, but you couldn't feel them.

The leaves in the hedgerow made a dry, scratchy noise as they scuttled about in its wake. The hedgerow itself rustled, as if filled with a thousand little occupants. The branches of the nearby trees creaked as they bent and strained.

The bodiless wind intensified and the sounds increased, like a discordant symphony. In the points where each noise overlapped and collided, new sounds could be heard, created by the dissonance. Sally tilted her head and listened carefully.

At first she made out the consonants in the discordance, plosive sounds like cracking twigs. Then she caught the vowels, low and keening like the wind moaning through the branches. A voice was coming through. A composite voice, like a thousand voices talking all at once and not one of them human.

"You have the—have the—have the meat—the meat—the meat . . . ?" said the voice.

"Yes," said Sally, clutching her bag.

She sensed the presence behind the voice, pictured it peering out from the shadows of the thicket. Something so primordial she could barely understand, let alone see.

"That is good—is good—is good. We can trap—can trap—can trap the Beast tonight."

Then, as sudden as a freak change in the weather, the wind disappeared, the trees and bushes stopped shaking, and Sally was alone.

She felt, as she always did when Hettie came and went, that a shadow had lifted from the sun. That the unreal had withdrawn and the real had rushed back in to fill the void it left. More worrying was the emptiness she felt, and the craving for Hettie's return.

Hettie was the name the townsfolk gave to the voice, and the inhuman presence that lurked behind it. Hettie of the Hedgerow. Sally had learned this from the pamphlet Jane had given her.

Increasingly, Sally felt her certainty wane whenever Hettie left—the sense of purpose Hettie instilled in Sally always seemed to ebb. For a second

Sally wavered and wondered if she was doing the right thing, and then she thought of David, and why the house was empty, and she realised she had to see this course of action through.

Sally hurried inside the cottage to prepare the meat.

CHAPTER 3

SALLY DROPPED LEAVES and berries into an old stone mortar. She'd collected them in the dark places Hettie had shown her in the forest on the hill that overlooked the cottage.

Sally pounded the mixture into a dense green pulp with a pestle, and laid out the steaks on the kitchen counter. She scooped out the pulp and massaged it into each of the steaks as though she were seasoning them, preparing a meal for the Beast, just as Hettie had instructed her.

It never felt like Sally was in the real world whenever she spoke with Hettie. It was as if someone had drawn back a curtain and given her a little glimpse of a world beyond her everyday existence, one that, for the sake of her sanity, she could only visit for a short time.

When she first heard Hettie speak, a few weeks ago, Sally realised she'd been picking up bits of her voice for quite a while. It wasn't anything she could put her finger on, merely a pattern in the noises she'd heard in the hedgerows around the cottage.

The more she started to identify the pattern, the more certain she became that there was a conscious presence behind it, something that was trying to make contact with her. Of course, Sally had no way of knowing, at first, whether this was all in her mind. There was never anyone with her when the pattern occurred, so she couldn't check if someone else had also heard it.

Twigs would snap in the hedgerow right next to her, and then again with her next step, and then again and again, keeping pace with her as she walked the length of the hedgerow. If she stopped, the snapping would stop, but as soon as she started walking, it would resume.

The first time this happened, Sally couldn't believe it. She was walking through the fields on her way to the forest. She knelt down and peered under the hedge, looking to see if there was a hedgehog or a bird there. All she saw was an intense darkness lurking just below the bushes. She couldn't see anything moving, but she still felt a presence, a brooding intelligence that didn't belong under a bush, or in a field, or anywhere in the world Sally knew.

She stood up very quickly and walked as far away from the hedge as she could. She felt like a field mouse whose fur has just been brushed by an owl's talon, filled with panic and a need to find shelter. She returned home as quickly as she could.

Sally avoided going to the forest for a whole week after that. She moped around the cottage, feeling bored. Apart from looking after David, she had nothing to do except read a book or visit Dunballan, and she never really enjoyed that. So she told herself not to be so stupid, that there was nothing under the hedgerow except a bird that had hopped away, then she put on her coat and went out.

Nothing happened on that walk, or the next two times she visited the forest, but the twig snapping soon returned and was joined, very shortly, by a strange breeze. It seemed to only blow down the length of the hedgerow and nowhere else in the field, rustling the branches and stirring the leaves underneath.

Like the twig snapping, the breeze and the leaf rustling kept time with Sally as she walked—it died down when she stood still and started up again when she continued. However much Sally avoided the hedges, as soon as she got near one she'd hear the regular sounds of twigs cracking and leaves scuttling.

Then she started to hear dripping. It didn't matter whether it had just rained or not, Sally would hear drops of liquid hitting the ground beneath the bushes and the shrubs. The liquid sometimes sounded a little heavier and thicker than water. She wasn't sure if it was sap or some other fluid that formed at the centre of the hedges.

The drips always fell in their own little rhythm, as though they were striking a counterpoint to the breaking of the twigs and the movement of the leaves, as though something were orchestrating all these noises according to its own dark design.

It was the fact that this only ever happened when Sally was by herself that really began to worry her. When David was able to join her, nothing happened in the hedgerows. She went into denial about what was happening, and blocked out the sound whenever she was near a hedge.

She told herself it was just a response to the strain of the move, that the isolation and loneliness she felt in the cottage—all by herself for days—was taking its toll. She was letting her imagination get the better of her, projecting her thoughts and fancies onto perfectly natural phenomenon.

She even made herself believe that for a while, until she heard a new pattern in the noises the hedgerow made. A pattern so carefully orchestrated it sounded like speech, not human speech, but something speaking in a language she understood.

"Little . . . sister-sister-sister . . . " it said.

It confirmed her worst fears. Up until that moment she'd only suspected she was going mad, but here was full blown proof that she'd lost her sanity. It's hard to deny your psychosis when you start hearing voices, even if those voices aren't human. Sally had given up a lot to move to Dunballan, but she didn't want to lose her mind. David depended on her too much to let that happen.

She avoided anywhere that had hedges for a long time after that, fields, open spaces, even her own garden. Sally refused to give in to the madness. If she could just stay away from it, she told herself, it might never find her again. Then she went into the library and everything changed.

CHAPTER 4

SALLY HAD POPPED into the library to cheer herself up. A coffee-morning at the community centre had emptied the place of pensioners and Jane was all by herself behind the desk. She waved Sally over when she saw her come in.

"I have something for you," Jane said.

Sally wasn't too sure about this, she didn't feel like chatting with Jane, but she was excited to see what Jane might have picked out for her, it might be an Audrey Niffenegger or a new Jennifer Egan she hadn't read. Jane nipped into the back room and appeared a moment later with a thick, green pamphlet.

"I think you might find this very interesting," she said, handing it to Sally.

Sally found it hard to mask her disappointment. "Oh," was all she could say looking at the battered green cover. It had an old woodcut on the front, showing a hare by a riverside, looking up at a smiling moon. The title, printed in crude block letters, was *Highways, Havens and Highlands* by James Hendry.

"It's by a local author," Jane said. "He was my uncle actually. He collected local folklore. He was hoping to get it published nationally or at least for the local tourist trade, but he couldn't resist putting in a few things about our little town. Local legends and such, and well, you know how secretive folk are around here. There were objections, and in the end he just had a few copies printed for private circulation. A shame, because it's really rather good. Anyway, I really think you'll find it . . . educational. What with . . . what with living here and everything . . . " Jane tried to smile. "You don't have to check it out. It's from my own private collection. Just get it back to me when you can." She was looking up at Sally with one of her awful, earnest expressions.

Sally put the pamphlet in her handbag. She glanced at the new arrivals shelf and the Recommended Reads, but she'd gone off the idea of browsing. "Thanks, Jane," she said. "I'll look at it later." Then she left, quite certain that she'd never once glance at the stupid thing.

The pamphlet sat for a couple of days under a pile of old magazines on the dining room table. Sally didn't bother to go back to the library—she found a box of old crime books from the 50s and 60s in the attic, and she made do with them. Finally the pamphlet got transferred to the recycling.

It stayed there for a week with the old newspapers and empty tins, until Sally decided to have a tidy up. David was having one of his 'episodes,' as she'd taken to calling them, and Sally was in a righteous fury, purging the cottage of junk.

The pamphlet must have fallen from a pile of newspapers on the way to the car. It wasn't until Sally came back from dropping off the recycling that she saw it lying on the floor of the hall. She picked it up and stared quizzically at it until she remembered where it had come from.

Her first reaction was irritation. Then she began to turn the pages and, despite the poor quality of the printing, it intrigued her. Sally made herself a cup of tea and settled down on the living room couch to read it.

There were chapters on hauntings, witchcraft, and faery folk that were local to the area. The chapter that really caught Sally's attention contained a story about the Gaelic Teine Biorach, a series of Will o' the Wisp sightings, and finally her heart raced when she read this passage:

"In addition to the Will o' the Wisp and our Gaelic equivalent the Teine Biorach, who traditionally haunt the marshes, our Highland hills have been home to many otherworldly visitors, who sometimes choose the most unique places to inhabit.

In the small town of Dunballan, the locals tell stories of a strange presence that haunts the thickets and hedgerows. No-one has ever seen this mysterious entity. They've only ever heard its voice, and a frightening voice it is at that, for it is said to sound like no human voice ever did. Those who've heard it describe it as sounding like, 'old leaves and twigs being crunched up' or 'lots of little pixies, all talking at once.' The locals call this eerie voice 'Hettie of the Hedgerow,' and claim she is either an ancient spirit, or a daemon from another realm. She is drawn to those in the depths of despair, and she often gives dire warnings which you would be foolish to ignore.

This can be seen in the earliest surviving tale of Hettie, from the late eighteenth century. A Poacher, who couldn't pay his fines, fled the bailiffs and hid in a ditch near Dunballan. In deep despair over his future, the Poacher called out to God to relieve him of his misery. God didn't answer him, but a voice from the hedgerow did.

Hettie told him to fashion a bow and arrow and to go deep into the old forest near Dunballan. Here he would find a maiden doe by a stream, which he was to shoot and to take to market the next day in Dunballan. The Poacher did as Hettie told him. He found the deer, shot it, and took its meat to market. The meat was so tender and sweet, it was said to bewitch all who tasted it. The Poacher sold all his wares for a premium and returned to the same hedgerow to ask for Hettie's help.

Hettie agreed to his pleas but cautioned him against ever growing horns himself, lest he come to a very bad end. The Poacher did not understand Hettie's warning, but he did follow her directions and once again bagged a prime maiden doe. He took the doe to market and even more people fell under the spell of its succulent meat. Soon, his hunting expeditions were proving so profitable that the Poacher not only paid off all his fines, he even opened a butcher's shop in Dunballan and took a young Wife.

His Wife was not faithful though and, unbeknownst to the Poacher, took a young Lover for herself. The poacher sold many types of meat in his shop, but people still clamoured for his venison. Because of this, the young Wife begged him to go and hunt more venison and to take her Lover with him. At first the Poacher refused. He had grown tired of asking for Hettie's help, but his Wife would not let up and wore him down with her moods and nagging, till eventually he relented.

After consulting privately with Hettie, the Poacher took his wife's Lover into the forest to hunt for deer. The poacher and his wife's lover became separated in the deep, dense forest and lost sight of each other. The Lover saw what he took to be a giant stag, he drew his bow, shot at it and his arrow landed true. When he came to claim his prize however, the Lover saw that he had not shot a stag, but had mistakenly killed the Poacher with his arrow.

The Poacher had failed to heed Hettie's warnings. He had grown cuckold's horns and as a consequence he had come to a very bad end at the hands of his young wife's Lover.

A later tale tells of a young Woman from Dunballan who took herself off to the forest to end her own life. The cause of her misery was the Laird of Dunballan, who had cast her aside and gone back to his wife as soon as she had given in to his attentions. With her honour in tatters, and her name besmirched, the Woman had vowed to end it all.

As she approached the forest, an otherworldly voice called to her from the hedgerow and asked why she was so sad. The Woman was taken aback, but confessed she could live with the shame she had brought on herself, but what she couldn't live with was the neglect the Laird had shown her.

Hettie told the Woman to go to a clearing in the forest and there she would find a hare. She was to kill the hare and bring it back with her. When the Woman had done this, Hettie told her how to prepare the hare with special herbs. Then she instructed the

Woman to take the hare to the Laird's manor and to have the Laird and his wife eat it. Hettie cautioned her against letting the smoke or flames of Elm tree wood come into contact with the hare's flesh while it was cooking.

The Woman took the hare to the manor and bribed the cook into serving the hare to the Laird and his wife. She made him promise not to use any elm tree wood in the fire. She did not extract that promise from the young kitchen hand though, and the boy used wood from the single Elm tree in the grounds of the manor to stoke the fire.

Once the Laird and his Wife had eaten the hare, the Wife took sick and died quite suddenly. Instead of mourning her death, the Laird became obsessed with the young Woman he had seduced and spurned. He pursued her doggedly and did not give up until the Woman agreed to be his new bride.

The marriage was not a happy one, however, for soon after they were wed, the Laird fell prey to the 'Curse of the McCavendish family' and neglected the Woman far more as his wife than when she was his spurned mistress. Unable to face this terrible outcome, the Woman hanged herself from the branches of the Elm tree in the grounds of the manor.

For more on the 'Curse of the McCavendish family' and Hettie's part in all this, see the section on the 'Beast of Dunballan' in the next chapter.

Reading this, Sally skipped ahead to the relevant section in the next chapter. What she read there opened her eyes. She saw how complicit everyone in Dunballan was in what was happening to David, including Jane. Hhow complicit they were in Sally's own suffering.

This enraged her more than anything ever had in her life, and when the initial storm of her anger had passed, it hardened into a cool, livid purpose. Without knowing it, Jane had also given Sally the answer to all of her problems.

Sally walked out of the cottage and into the nearby field. She stood by the long hedgerow and took a deep breath.

"Alright then," she said. "Talk to me."

There was a brief pause where nothing happened. Sally felt very self-conscious—she'd just spoken to a row of bushes. What if it really was all in her mind?

It was with a huge relief that she heard a few disparate twigs cracking beneath the hedge. The breeze came again, only this time it was stronger. It didn't only shake the hedge's branches, but also rippled the grass at Sally's feet and lifted her hair. It bent the branches of the trees by the hedge and excited all the leaves beneath it.

There was no substance to the breeze. Sally did not feel the air move, she only saw the things around her in motion, including her own billowing jacket. It looked like wind but it did not feel like it. It was an entirely different phenomenon altogether.

It didn't sound like wind either. As it intensified, it gave off a low, keening moan that started to modulate its frequency. More twigs snapped like little fire crackers going off beneath the thicket, and the leaves rattle and danced.

Sally strained her ears for a pattern. The noises of the leaves and twigs began to order themselves as though they were mimicking a tongue, teeth and lips. The varying pitch of the wind seemed to solidify into vowels, and a voice came through. The voice that Sally had heard before.

She wasn't hallucinating, she couldn't be. No human mind could bend these sounds into such a complex symphony. Something utterly inhuman was talking to her.

"You are not alone—not alone—not alone anymore—anymore—anymore." Hettie said.

Sally swallowed and her eyes misted over. She blinked and a tear ran down one cheek. "Really?" she said. "I really don't have to face this on my own now?"

"We're here to give you—give you—give you back what the Beast—what the Beast—what the Beast has stolen."

"You better not be lying to me," Sally said. She bit her bottom lip and clenched her hands into fists. "Because if you are, I don't care how old you are, I swear to God I'll kill you."

Sally was surprised at how fierce her reaction was. An unearthly voice had addressed her. An inhuman presence beneath the bushes of the hedgerow had reached out and made contact. Yet she didn't doubt her sanity, and she wasn't afraid.

Instead, Sally felt something she hardly dared accept, something she hadn't felt since moving to the remote Highland town. She felt solidarity. It had seemed, since arriving in Dunballan, that everything was against her, not just the townsfolk, freezing her out with their appropriation of David, or even the landscape and the ancient forest above the hill, but also some unseen, primal force that imposed itself on them all.

Now Sally had a strange phenomenon all of her own, something to counteract the unknown powers she was up against. One that understood her predicament and wanted to help.

"You want to take—to take—to take back your man—your man—your man."

"And you'll help me?"

"We will school you—school you—school you, little sister."

"So, there is a way to fix this, to release him I mean?"

"You can release him—release him—release him, but you must never try—never try—never try to unlock him."

Sally wondered if Hettie was giving her a warning or relationship advice. She had wanted to unlock David practically as long as she'd known him, but she'd always been afraid of the consequences.

CHAPTER 5

DISTANCE HAD ALWAYS been a feature of Sally and David's relationship, both physically and emotionally. In the ten years they'd been together they'd never lived in the same property, not until they moved to Dunballan. When they were in London they lived in separate flats in totally different parts of the city, at least half an hour's bus ride from one another.

They weren't the sort of people who made connections easily and neither of them had a large circle of friends. Sally had only had two other lovers and David assured her he hadn't had many more. He refused to be more specific than that, and Sally had learned not to press him.

They were comfortable with their remoteness, neither of them wanting to cling to the other or make any demands. Sally had been fiercely independent since she was a child, and she hated to be dependent on anyone or have anyone depend on her. Several days could go by without Sally or David contacting the other, and it wouldn't worry them in the slightest. They were happy being self-contained, and their relationship seemed stronger because of it.

Or it did in the beginning.

Looking back on their last year in London, Sally couldn't help but see a certain inevitability to the way they drifted apart. The one thing they'd seen as the biggest strength of their relationship was ultimately its undoing. They spent so long ensuring they didn't need each other too much that they came to wonder if they needed each other at all.

David's depression had been getting steadily worse for quite some time. When he was made redundant he went into a sharp decline. His firm gave him a generous settlement. He didn't have any monetary problems, but he depended on work to keep his black moods at bay. He needed to remain active and stay one step ahead of them.

In the past, David liked having Sally around when he got down, just knowing she was there had helped, but this time he found her presence a torment. He froze her out and went weeks without seeing her. Sally began to blame herself—she must be lacking in some way or David wouldn't treat her like this. Every time she reached out to him, he pulled further away. She began to despair of having any connection with him at all.

Just when she thought things couldn't get any worse, David received news that changed everything. An elderly uncle died and left his entire estate to him. Sally knew his family were once well-to-do, but she hadn't known David was the sole heir. The inheritance came with one major stipulation, in order to claim the estate, David would have to go and live in his ancestral home.

Sally felt sure this would be the end of their relationship, so she was shocked when David called, out of the blue, to invite her out to dinner. He took her to an Italian restaurant she really liked in Islington, and ordered an expensive bottle of wine.

"So," he said, as they waited for their main course. "I had the estate agents round today. They think they can get me a pretty good price for the flat."

"Oh really?" she said, and suddenly her appetite disappeared. She was used to David's insensitivity, but this was a bit much even for him. She knew she was going to lose him, and she was trying to prepare herself for this, but he didn't have to start bragging about how much money he was going to make from the move.

"The thing is, they have an office in your neck of the woods and, when I mentioned your place to them, they sounded quite interested."

"I don't think I can afford to move, not with stamp duty and everything, and I'd probably end up with somewhere smaller than I've got now."

"Not if you moved out of London, you wouldn't."

"Why on earth would I want to move out of London?"

"Well, you'd have to if you were going to move in with me. I mean, if you wanted to, in my cottage in the Highlands, that is. There aren't too many mod cons, but it's quite roomy."

Sally put down her glass in shock. "Are you asking me to move in with you?"

"If you want to, I mean we have been together for quite a while now. It does seem like the logical thing to do."

This was the last thing she'd expected David to say. Sally didn't know how she felt about it. Or to be more exact, she was feeling so many things at once her emotions had gotten caught in a log jam, and she had no idea whether she was anxious or elated, flattered or stunned.

Sally was quite a deliberate person, and she didn't make snap decisions. Being put on the spot like this usually sent her into a tailspin of indecision. So she was completely caught off guard to hear a calm, clear voice say, "I'd love to." And even more caught off guard when she realised it was her own.

With hindsight, Sally wondered if her voice would have been quite so clear or calm if she'd known exactly what would happen when they did move.

CHAPTER 6

FIRST WEEKS IN DUNBALLAN:

DAVID HAD NO problem selling his apartment, it was snapped up after only a few viewings. He sold most of his other possessions and was ready to move in a matter of months.

Sally did not have it so easy. She found a buyer, but got caught up in a property chain that dragged on interminably and seemed like it would never be resolved. She would have pulled out and put her flat back on the market, but the buyer was offering her so much over the asking price that she didn't want to lose him.

She gave notice at the primary school where she worked as a teacher, but there wasn't time to find a similar position in or around Dunballan.

"I've no idea what I'm going to do for an income," she said to David over the phone, soon after he'd left for Dunballan. "Maybe I should wait a bit before coming up, at least until I've sold my flat."

"No, don't do that." There was a hint of alarm in David's voice that wasn't like him, nor was the needy undertone. "I've got quite a bit set aside, more than enough to tide us both over."

"But I don't want to be dependent on you for money. You're already giving me a place to stay."

"I'm not giving you a place to stay, we're moving in together. There's a difference, and if we're going to do it, we might as well do it properly. There's really no reason to put it off. It'll be much easier to find work once you're up here and you get to know the area."

"Are you sure?"

"Of course I'm sure." Then the subtle neediness crept back into his voice. "You're not getting cold feet are you?"

"No, of course not, it's just . . . well, we've spent ten years living apart, what difference will a few months make?"

"I miss you," he said, quite plainly. "And I need you here."

That was all he had to say. Sally dropped everything. She booked a train ticket and packed her bags the very next day. David had never openly said that to her before. After years of convincing themselves that they wanted to be together, but didn't need to be, and the months of slowly growing apart, it meant everything for David to reach out to her like that.

It was only later that she discovered why he really needed her at Dunballan.

Sally arrived with only a few boxes of possessions, having sold everything else she owned in an act of extreme de-cluttering. All she kept was the bare minimum to set up home with David. When she arrived at the six bedroom cottage, Sally found there was nowhere to put any of her things.

The cottage had six full dinner services, three sets of silver cutlery, and enough antique furniture and fittings to fill a warehouse. David's uncle had fancied himself a gourmet cook and had packed the kitchen with every imaginable gadget. Sally ended up storing her stuff in the already crowded attic.

The fixtures and fittings might not have been to Sally's taste, but she had fun doing the place up with David and living out her renovation fantasies. The garden was a huge luxury. There was room for a small orchard, a large lawn and even an allotment at the bottom where they'd planned to grow vegetables.

They took long walks together over the hills of the surrounding valley and into the forest just beyond their cottage. When the long winter nights came in, they drank Shiraz and stared into the freshly lit fire, trying to catch a vision of their future in the flames that leaped in the hearth.

"How does small town living suit you then?" said David, one night, as he stirred the embers and added a new log. "Have we converted the city girl yet?"

"I'm not sure, it's all a bit . . . I don't know, claustrophobic isn't it?"

David's face fell and a touch of nervousness crept into his voice. "You don't like it?"

"I didn't say that," Sally said, trying to reassure him. "I love the cottage and the countryside and everything, I'm just not used to being under such scrutiny, that's all. Everyone seems to want to know everything about us. You must have noticed."

"Yes, we are the subject of a lot of gossip, like we're local celebrities or something."

"Dunballan's own Will and Kate."

David laughed. "You're happy, though?"

"Yes, I am, how about you? Your spirits seem to have lifted since you got here."

"They have. It's quite surprising really, I feel far

more at home than I thought I would, like some burden's been lifted off me or something."

Sally took his hand and kissed it. "Thank you," she said.

"For what?"

"For including me in your life, for making me an integral part of it. You know my family history, I was always on the outside. I feel like I've been on the outside most of my life, but you brought me up here with you and included me in your plans. That means a lot."

"Does it?"

"Probably more than you'll ever know."

She was happy in that moment, happier than she'd been in a long while. She had so many hopes for their future together.

Then the Beast came along and ruined everything.

CHAPTER 7

THE FIRST TIME THE BEAST CAME:

DAVID SAW THE Beast first. He always did. It was like he was attuned to it, connected on some deep hereditary level.

It took Sally a little while to realise that he was looking at something. They would usually be outside, near the house or the forest, and David would go quiet all of a sudden and stare into the distance. Sally would spot the change in his mood—since moving in with him she'd become acutely aware of the shifts in David's temperament.

She let it go the first few times, presuming he'd paused for thought and, if he wanted to share what he was thinking, he would. She didn't like to pry, and she knew David still needed his own space. She'd come to expect a certain level of intimacy with him since moving in. She knew he had his own interior life and she respected that, but she didn't want to be left out entirely. She began to scrutinise him when his gaze wandered, and she realised he was looking at something specific.

"What have you spotted?" she asked him eventually. They were working on the allotment at the time. Sally was sowing runner beans, pushing them into loose trenches of soil while David cut bamboo canes.

"What?"

"I asked what you'd spotted."

"Had I spotted something?"

"I don't know, you tell me."

David paused for a moment, then held up the cane he'd just cut. "Do you think these are long enough? I wasn't certain how big the frames should be. How long do the shoots grow, anyway?"

Every time Sally caught him looking at something in the distance, David would smile and shake his head in a self-conscious way, and then try and change the subject. Sally had a feeling that whatever was drawing his attention was getting closer and closer. She was right, and finally she caught sight of it.

They were coming back from a walk and were almost at the garden gate. David stood stock-still and shuddered, as if from a sudden chill. He turned to look up at the woods on the hill. Sally looked too and there, between two trees on the edge of the bluff, she saw a huge, black, feline creature.

The creature disappeared back into the trees so quickly that Sally wasn't sure she'd seen it. If David hadn't been staring at the same place, she might have dismissed it. David had seen it too though, she knew he had.

"What on earth was that?" she said.

"What?" David looked startled, guilty even, as if he'd been caught doing something he shouldn't.

"Up there on the rise."

"Come on, it's going to be dark soon. We should get inside." David turned and started back to the cottage.

"I know you saw it," Sally said. "I saw you looking at it. You spotted it before I did."

David continued to walk away from her.

"David . . . " she called after him.

"We need to get back," was all he said.

As soon as they got back in the house, David went straight to his study and shut the door. When Sally knocked, he called out "I'm busy" and didn't bother to open up. She was puzzled by this behavior. David could be secretive and self-contained at times, but she'd never seen such outright denial from him.

It would have been easy to draw a line under the incident and forget it had ever happened. To write the whole thing off as an anomaly, but the Beast kept appearing—it wouldn't leave David alone.

They were foraging for chanterelle mushrooms a week or so later. David remembered doing it with his grandfather many years before. The idea of foraging really appealed to them, living off the land and filling their larder with wild produce.

The only problem was they were hopeless at it. After several hours they'd only found a handful of fungi and they didn't know if any of them were edible or not. The tiny pictures in the field guide they'd brought along weren't at all helpful.

They were on the outskirts of the forest, and were about to call it a day when they heard twigs cracking a little farther off, where the trees were denser. They both looked up and saw a huge black shape pacing back and forth between the trees. It stopped, lifted its head as if scenting the air, and then slunk back into the forest.

"There," said Sally, much louder than she'd meant to. "You saw that didn't you? You saw it."

David, who was crouching over a rotting trunk, just stared down at the leaf mulch in front of him.

After that, the Beast didn't bother to hide itself as much. It became a lot more brazen, appearing closer and closer to their remote cottage. Each time she saw it, Sally was struck with how large it was. She guessed that its head would be level with her own, and the length of its body was that of an average pony.

Its legs and back were all compacted muscle, and it moved with a grace that didn't seem possible. Almost as if it was reforming itself with every movement, sinews and bone becoming liquid every time it lifted a paw, turning solid again only when it was still. The creature's coat was jet black—you couldn't make out a single hair in it. It wasn't glossy either, it was darker than anything Sally had ever seen, and the light seemed to fall into it.

Sally began to wonder if the Beast was what her former boyfriend, Malcolm, would have called an Alien Big Cat, or an ABC for short, one of the strange wildcats seen wandering the British countryside. Malcolm was a few years older than Sally and considered himself an expert in fringe studies—this included alternate history, conspiracy theory, and cryptozoology. He'd dropped out of university because he didn't like "being told what to think," and he wanted to devote himself to learning "the hidden truths behind modern history."

Sally found him intriguing at first. He was so sure of himself and his intelligence, in spite of working one dead end job after another. After a while though, she began to find his attempts to "de-programme her from all the misconceptions of consensus reality" both pedantic and tiresome.

One of Malcolm's pet topics was alien big cats. He kept a scrapbook filled with cuttings that mentioned sightings of large wildcats in remote places. One day he meant to write the definitive book on the subject but, like all of Malcolm's grand plans, it came to nothing in the end. Sally wondered if she ought to take a photo of the Beast on her phone and send it to Malcolm. She didn't have his contact details though—she hadn't spoken with him for years, and she wasn't sure she wanted to get back in touch.

Sally preferred to keep Malcolm and the Beast out of her relationship as much as possible. The Beast, however, had other ideas.

CHAPTER 8

SALLY BECAME LESS frightened of the Beast, but not less wary. It seemed to be less nervous of being seen, creeping closer and closer to the house.

She glimpsed it at the edge of the forest, coming a little farther out from the trees each time. Then she caught sight of it behind a hedgerow in the field next to her garden. Finally, while she was standing at the back door to the cottage, looking out over the gentle slope of the garden, she saw its long, sinuous tail flicking backwards and forwards over the top of the garden wall.

It never made the slightest noise and disappeared from view almost as soon as she saw it. Sally sometimes wondered if her eyes were playing tricks on her, but she knew David was aware of its presence too, even though he refused to acknowledge the Beast, let alone discuss it.

Sally took to leaving knives, axes, and anything else she could use as a weapon, around the cottage and garden, hidden in strategic places so she was never far from something she could use to defend herself. She was sure the Beast was stalking them and, as it came closer and closer, they'd find out what it wanted. Nothing, however, could have prepared her for what that was.

She didn't have to wait long to find out. One day, the Beast jumped over their garden wall and walked right up to the cottage.

Sally was tidying the back bedroom. She looked out of the window and saw it stalking up to the house. She called out to David and heard his footsteps on the stairs. She raced down after him to lock and bolt the back door but she found him there already. He had opened the door to the Beast. It was sitting on the stoop.

Sally froze in the kitchen doorway. "David," she said in a loud whisper. "What are you doing?" David didn't answer. He was too captivated by the Beast.

It looked patient and alert, resting on its back haunches. Its front legs were upright, and its tail was curved around in front of them. In spite of its immense size, it wasn't threatening, but it wasn't like any creature Sally had ever seen. The shape of its ears, its muzzle and its head gave the Beast an otherworldly air, like an infernal re-imagining of what a feline would look like.

Sally came a little closer. She didn't join David at the door, but remained a few steps behind, watching *him* more than the Beast. David did not look uneasy. He had the air of a man who has just confronted his wife and his mistress for the first time, and is relieved it's all out in the open. He looked at the creature like he was greeting an old friend. There was an obvious intimacy between him and the Beast, and Sally couldn't suppress a sudden, irrational surge of jealousy at the thought.

Sally pulled closer to David. He belonged to her, and she didn't trust the Beast one bit. The Beast paid her no attention—its eyes were on David and David's eyes were on the Beast.

The Beast opened its eyes wide, retracting its eyelids until its black, watery globes were like two distended orbs. David let out a little gasp, and Sally saw that his eyes were also wide open and bulging. He rocked up onto the balls of his feet and leaned forward, towards the Beast, holding its gaze the whole time.

The Beast rose slowly to its feet, never breaking eye contact with David. The two of them seemed to be swooning. David's breathing became shallower and more rapid. The Beast showed its formidable claws. They were long and pointed, yellow like ivory against the dark pelt of its paws. It dug the pointed end of the claws into the rough stone of the patio and scraped large grooves into it.

David seemed entranced and a low moan escaped the back of his throat. He was swaying on his feet, leaning closer and closer to the creature. The Beast stretched out its front legs, arched its spine and raised its hind quarters. Its tail stood erect, only the very end curled and uncurled as a deep, low purr rumbled from its chest.

A hot, thick scent filled the air around the door, a deep, musky odor that was at once bestial but contained smells that couldn't have come from anywhere in this world. Sally choked and covered her face, but David breathed it deeply in.

She turned to him, appalled at how he was behaving. "Stop it," she said, punching his arm. "Stop it! Stop it! Stop it!"

It did no good, David was oblivious. He leaned so far forward that he looked like he was going to topple over. His chest was rising and falling, and his arms shook like he was caught up in some kind of religious ecstasy.

Sally looked from the Beast to David and back again. The Beast's head was thrown back, and its body was tense, as though it was about to spring. Something about it was different though, something had changed.

It seemed to have something essential of David within it. As though his mind, and even his soul, had been transferred in that gaze, had leapt from his eyes and poured into the Beast's.

The Beast relaxed and stood still for a moment, all the tension drained from its body. It looked slowly about, getting its bearings. Sally could swear she detected some of David's manner about it, something indefinable in the way it moved. Almost as if it were copying his mannerisms in the way a huge wildcat might mimic the actions of a man.

Then the Beast turned from her and padded back down the garden. It jumped over the wall and bounded up to the forest, picking up speed as it went. Finally it was swallowed by the trees.

CHAPTER 9

SALLY TURNED BACK to David. His jaw was slack, his mouth hung open, and his eyes were empty and glazed.

Sally tried to rouse him. "David," she said. "David?" But he didn't respond. Sally passed her hand in front of his face. He didn't blink or show any expression. He was breathing through his mouth, deep, steady breaths that rattled the phlegm at the back of his throat. Sally took his hand and checked the pulse in his wrist—it was regular. He neither resisted nor responded to any of this.

His body was fine, but David himself appeared to be absent. Sally clicked her fingers next to his ear and shook his shoulders, but this didn't get any reaction. She raised her hand and slapped him hard about the face, hoping to shock him out of his stupor. She left a red mark on his cheek, but his vacant expression didn't alter a bit.

When she saw the mark, Sally regretted being so violent. She didn't want to hurt David, but she didn't know what else to do. She couldn't rouse him, and she was running out of options. He wasn't moving, but she couldn't leave him loitering by the back door, so she took hold of his shoulders and attempted to turn him around. He shifted quite compliantly, moving exactly where she wanted him to go. His face was blank and didn't respond in any way, but his basic motor functions were working fine.

Sally led David back to the living room and helped him sit in his favourite armchair. She spoke to him the whole while, as if she were guiding him blindfolded, but he didn't make any response. He remained in the chair for the rest of the day, breathing loudly through his mouth and blinking slowly.

Sally fed him soup for supper, spooning it into his mouth, and then took him up to bed. He had no problem with the stairs and was easy to undress, but he lay like an unmoving lump in the bed.

Every day Sally would get him out of bed, dress him, feed him porridge or broth, and bathe him when he needed it. She improvised a 'man diaper' from a few old towels and some safety pins, and she'd change it once a day. At night she would undress him and put him to bed.

Not once did he acknowledge her or anything else around him. He was just a heavy sack of flesh that had been left in the place of her partner. David was no longer with her in the cottage, not the David she knew and loved, and had allowed herself to become dependent on. The David who fascinated, engaged, and occasionally infuriated her. That David had left when the Beast came to call. He was running around somewhere in the forest inside the Beast.

While David answered the call of the wild, Sally was left to tidy up the mess that was left behind. Her life became one of drudgery, care giving, and loneliness. She tried all kinds of things to rouse

David—she played him music, going through all the playlists on his phone. She put on the television and talk radio, tuned to all his favourite sports and current affairs shows. None of it worked. He didn't respond to any type of stimulus. He just sat there, inert, doing nothing but breathe.

Many times Sally was ready to call the doctor, or an ambulance, driving out of Dunballan until she got a phone signal, but she never went through with it. She always hung up at the last minute. She knew she was being foolish, but she had no idea how she'd explain what had happened, not without sounding like she'd lost her mind. They'd probably take her in to see a psychiatrist, wondering if she'd snapped from the pressure of looking after David.

Sally could have lied, or simply told them she didn't know what had caused David's condition, but they'd want to take him away and do all sorts of tests on him. Sally was sure that David would snap out of it and come back to her at some point. She was worried that taking him too far away would endanger this. That if she let them take him to hospital, he wouldn't be able to find his way back to his body.

As miserable as David's day-to day-care made her, Sally could at least take comfort in the increased intimacy she had with him. This had its downsides, such as seeing to his toilet functions, but she got to fuss him a lot more, choose his wardrobe and touch him whenever she wanted, without any pretext. She could tend to his body, even if his soul was elsewhere, and she took some solace in that.

She also took solace in tending to her own soul, by returning to her Catholicism. Sally hadn't been to church since she came to Dunballan, not that she went regularly when she lived in London, but her faith had always been there in times of need. There was only one church in Dunballan, an old Presbyterian building on the high street that never opened its doors and didn't seem to have a congregation. Sally wasn't sure she would have gone even if it did hold services.

Sally's family weren't religious, but her mother had sent her to the local Catholic school because it had the best academic record in the area. Her mother would probably have shipped her off to boarding school if she could have afforded it. She had very little time for Sally when she was growing up, because she was too busy looking after her father.

Sally was never allowed to help with her father, or even to touch him. He received all her mother's attention and Sally was excluded from the whole process, just as she was excluded by the children at school.

Sally thought of her mother often, in those first days caring for David. She thought of what her mother must have gone through and how much like her she was becoming, now she had a man of her own to look after.

Would she turn out any better than her mother?

CHAPTER 10

BEFORE SALLY MET DAVID:

WHEN SHE WAS in her early twenties, Sally went to see a counsellor to work on the problems she had with intimacy and relationships.

Her name was Margaret. She was a large, middle-aged lady with grey hair and a weakness for silk scarves. She spent many sessions talking about Sally's early life, and her mother's second marriage, and then she offered Sally a prognosis.

"What I think," Margaret said, "is that the lack of connection you feel towards others is a defence mechanism. It's a way of protecting yourself from getting hurt."

Sally's father had suffered a massive cerebral haemorrhage when Sally was very young, which had left him incapacitated and unable to fend for himself. He became a shell of his former self, a slack-jawed, drooling lump whom Sally couldn't bear to be around most of the time.

Sally's mother became his full time caretaker, a task which left her emotionally and physically drained. She had no time for Sally when she was done with her husband. Sally was constantly shooed away, sent out to play or just told to leave her mother alone.

"You see yourself as unworthy of your mother's love and attention because you weren't ill like your father. You think that's why you were always left out."

Her father died when Sally was thirteen. He'd been dependent on her mother for nearly a decade. Sally was at a difficult age, and she and her mother rarely spoke. She hardly noticed when, some time later, her mother began seeing another man, a widower called Bert whom she'd met at a support group. He was younger than her mother and had two young daughters.

None of this mattered to Sally until her mother announced she was going to marry Bert and move in with him. Bert was a quiet, gentle man who mainly kept out of Sally's way, but his two daughters were a different matter. They sucked up to Sally's mother at every opportunity, and her mother loved it.

Her mother had always wanted more children, but her father's condition made that impossible.

"Your mother felt guilty about not being a better mother to you," Margaret told her. "She was compensating for this in the way she treated your stepsisters. They gave her the opportunity to be the mother she'd always wanted to be."

This didn't make Sally resent her any less, though. The care her mother showed her stepsisters made Sally feel every bit as excluded as the care she'd shown her father.

Sally left for university when she was nineteen and never returned home. She'd seen her mother on only three occasions since, and not a single thing between them was ever resolved.

"The reason you remain distant from others is

because you're frightened of being hurt. Your relationship with your mother taught you that intimacy leads to exclusion. You can't bear the thought of being excluded like your parents excluded you. That's why you seek false comfort in emotional dead-ends like Catholicism."

Margaret, it turned out, wasn't any more religious than Sally's mother. That's why Sally finally stopped seeing her, or at least that's what she told herself. If Sally was honest, she stopped going because Margaret was forcing her to face up to too many truths, and she wasn't able to accept them just yet.

All this played on Sally's mind as she looked after David and tended to his needs. It brought back lots of things from her childhood that she'd either forgotten or purposefully buried. One incident in particular came back to her with a sudden and terrible force.

CHAPTER 11

When Sally was around nine years old, her mother had walked into the living room to find Sally, with her hands on her father's head and her eyes closed, praying to God in a loud voice. Sally had seen a film in morning assembly about Saints and the healing power of faith, so she'd been inspired to try it on her father.

She was sure that her father's soul was still out there, caught somewhere between Heaven and Earth, waiting to return to his body. Sally wanted God to reach up and pull her father's soul back into his body, so he could open his eyes and be his old self again. She was certain that God could do that if only she believed it hard enough and prayed as loud as she could.

She was praying so loudly that she didn't hear her mother come into the room to see why she was making so much noise. The first she knew of her mother's presence was the sharp stinging pain she felt as her mother slapped her hands away from her father.

"What on earth do you think you're playing at?" her mother demanded. Her face was stern and angry. "You know you're not supposed to touch your father. You're going to give him a fit with all that shouting."

Sally rubbed her hands as her eyes filled up with

tears. "I wasn't shouting, Mummy, I was praying. I was asking God to help Daddy."

Some of the anger left her mother's face, but she was just as stern. "I don't believe in God, darling, He doesn't exist, and even if he did, there isn't a thing he could do for your father I'm afraid. Now you know I don't like you bothering him."

"You never let me help you?"

"That's because he's my responsibility, not yours. You're just a child. I don't want you taking this burden on."

"But I want to help, Mummy, and so does God."

"I've already told you god doesn't exist!"

"Mummy, it's a sin to say that, you mustn't say that."

"Don't be so silly, I can say what I like."

"But it's a sin, and Father Murphy told us it says in the Bible that 'the sins of the father will be visited upon the children,' and that goes for mummies too, because Susan Brown asked him if it did and he said 'yes.' And if you don't believe in God then I'll get punished."

"Don't be so ridiculous." Her mother's brow furrowed. "Of course you won't have to pay for my sins, there's no such thing as sin. Just as there isn't any God, not for me and certainly not for your poor father."

Sally began to cry much harder. Her mother was really scaring her. She'd never heard her speak this way about God before. Sally assumed her mother accepted God the same way all her teachers at school did. She had no idea there were adults who didn't believe in Him.

"But Mummy, how can you live in a world without God?" She wanted to know if such a thing were even possible. She couldn't think of anything more frightening.

Her mother saw she was scaring Sally and did what she always did when she hurt or upset her daughter—she pulled away. She turned back to Sally's father and began to fuss with his hair, where Sally had touched it, avoiding Sally's eyes.

"Really, Sally, you're upsetting your father with all that fuss. You know how sensitive he is. I've told you time and time again that we mustn't disturb him. You're going to have to take yourself off to your room until you calm down." Her mother pointed to the door. "Go on," she said.

Sally was only trying to help her father. She couldn't understand why her mother was being so cruel. It didn't seem fair. She tried to get control of herself, but she only cried harder.

Her father didn't seem the least bit affected by Sally's crying, for all her mother's protests. He just stared ahead with his mouth open, his only movement the rise and fall of his chest. He never reacted to anything anymore, that's why Sally had prayed for him. Sally couldn't see the harm in that.

Even still, her mother hadn't relented, and she'd sent Sally from the room.

Looking back, Sally could understand why her mother had said those things to her. She was using Sally's father to avoid having a relationship with God, just as she was using him to avoid having a relationship with Sally.

Sally's father had come to dominate her mother's life. She had long ago let go of the hope that he would get better and come back to her. She accepted him for what he'd become. He was like a living statue of a minor deity, and her mother had to make constant and continual offerings to him. There was no room in her life for any other God.

Looking after David had allowed Sally to understand many things about her mother. She could appreciate why she was so withdrawn and where her moods had come from. She saw her mother's actions with an adult's eye, and she came to realise she wasn't responsible for her mother's behaviour, it hadn't been her fault. It had just been the situation her mother was in.

None of this helped her to forgive her mother. She wasn't ready for that yet. Sally had decided she would cope with her situation much better than her mother had.

She would not lose her relationship with God. She would not let go of her hope that David would come back to her.

CHAPTER 12

THE FIRST TIME THE BEAST LEFT:

SALLY'S HOPE WAS repaid one afternoon, around two weeks after the Beast first appeared.

She wasn't aware of the actual time it occurred because she was busying herself with chores. David was in the conservatory, a cluttered room with large, single glazed windows at the back of the cottage. The room was something of a dumping ground. They kept the recycling in there, along with an assortment of gardening tools and some old rattan furniture.

Sally had found no effective way of bringing David out of his torpor, so she'd taken to leaving him in the conservatory. He was out from under her feet and she hoped that when the sun came out, he'd at least enjoy the feel of it on his face.

She was in the kitchen, which was also at the back of the cottage, washing the dishes and staring out across the garden, wondering what else she should try and plant in the flower beds. Something caught her eye at the very end of the garden, just beyond the wall. It looked like a long, black snake at first, but it was standing up in the air, waving about.

Sally realised it wasn't a snake—it was the end of a tail. She peered more closely, but it seemed to have disappeared. She left the sink and went to the conservatory which had more windows and a better view of the garden.

Sally couldn't see anything from the conservatory, just a couple of crows on the wall that were eyeing the beans she'd planted. She shook her head and decided she was either mistaken or her eyes were playing tricks on her.

She was drying her hands on the front of her slacks when she heard someone clear their throat behind her. Sally froze, her mind raced. She was all alone out here. What if someone had broken in?

"Could I have a glass of water," a voice said. Sally was so surprised she let out a cry of alarm, and then she recognised the voice as David's.

She turned to look at him, sitting in the rattan chair behind her. He blinked rapidly several times and smiled apologetically.

"I'm sorry," he said. "My throat's rather dry."

CHAPTER 13

SALLY ROOTED AROUND in the back of the kitchen cupboard until she found the largest Tupperware box she had.

She put the box on the counter and filled it with all the steaks, each one seasoned, and then marinated as Hettie had instructed. The steaks had been cut into rough chunks and smelled quite strongly of the marinade. Sally was actually glad to get the lid on the Tupperware box.

Next she fetched David's old Zippo with the Boy Scout emblem on it, and a bottle of paraffin. Then she went and got the small wooden box that had been sitting on the crowded mantelpiece in the living room. It had a strange carving of a tree on the lid. Sally wasn't an expert in trees, but it looked like an elm tree. Around the base of the trunk was a cage with its gate open. Just what this meant, or why anyone would want to cage a tree, Sally didn't know, but she thought it would be a perfect container for the figurine.

She'd made the figurine this morning out of all the hair she'd collected in the box last night, weaving it together with thread until she had a pretty good likeness. The wooden box turned out to be exactly the right size, and the figurine fitted it just fine. Finally she got a two-kilogram bag of salt and the last few volumes of the journals she'd found in David's study. She'd carried most of the journals to the forest already, but she couldn't take them all in one go.

When she was done, she went and got her coat, put everything except the Tupperware box into a big cloth bag, picked it all up and left by the back door. She tried not to look at the neglected garden as she headed towards the back gate. Spring would arrive soon, the life would come back into her garden and she would have someone to help her get it into shape.

Sally left the garden and began to climb the hill that led up to the forest, keeping close to the large hedgerow that ran up one side. She listened very closely for any breeze or movement in the thicket. Twice she stood dead still, convinced she heard some movement in the shrubs, but each time she was mistaken and no presence made itself known.

The hedge came to an end around three-quarters of the way up the hill where it met another hedge at the far corner of a field. Sally was feeling a little deflated as she passed it, but her spirits rose when she heard a sudden commotion.

The thicket shook, as if someone had taken hold of it by force. The branches creaked and scraped each other and, in the darkest part of the undergrowth, something stirred up the dead leaves. From this cacophony of overlapping noises, a brittle, unnatural voice emerged.

"Nearly ready now—ready now—ready now. Everything is in place—is in place—is in place. The Beast will not last the night—last the night—last the night!"

Sally drummed her fingers on the Tupperware box. As usual, whenever Hettie appeared, she felt her pain, anguish, and despondency disappear into the darkness beneath the hedgerow.

"It's really going to be over?" she said, hopefully.

"You have done all we asked—all we asked—all we asked, the trap has been most carefully laid—carefully laid—carefully laid."

The hedgerow stilled and the voice grew silent. Sally already regretted it, already longed for Hettie's return. As if in answer to this, the bodiless breeze left the hedgerow and beat a path through the long grass, bending the stalks and parting the weeds, as if leading her up to the forest. Sally followed it with an almost childlike eagerness.

The trees were sparser around the outskirts of the forest and also more varied. There were native sessile oaks and silver birches, and the ground was covered with bluebells throughout spring and early summer. Deeper into the forest, where the trees were denser, the Caledonian pines were dominant.

The earth was cooler up at this height and the air cleaner. Sally could never decide what the forest smelled like. The deeper you went, the more the resinous scent of the pines held sway. Further out, this was undercut by the rich loamy aromas of the forest floor and, just when you got used to that, there were sudden, sweet bursts of wildflowers.

The forest had been a haven for Sally when they first arrived. Like a beacon on the hill behind their cottage, it seemed to have been calling her all the way from London. No matter how claustrophobic small town life became, the forest was always her refuge, her justification for moving.

But it hadn't been calling to her at all, it had been calling David. Sally was simply caught up in his slipstream. What had once seemed so magical to her was now ruined by the Beast. This was where it took him.

Sally couldn't look at a tree trunk, a wildflower, or a fallen branch without wondering if David had seen it through the Beast's eyes. Everywhere bore the taint of its presence and the theft of her man. Walking through the forest now was like walking through the bedroom of David's mistress, while the sheets were still crumpled and warm with betrayal.

Sally would have been able to bear it better if he'd only talk to her about what had happened. She was desperate to know what went on when he was with the Beast, but David always shut down whenever she broached the subject. She tried approaching it gently, asking indirect questions, giving him openings in the conversation, but he never responded.

It seemed so unfair, they'd come so far, opened up so much to each other since moving to Dunballan. Why was he closing down on her now? Surely he owed her some explanation, some sense of what was happening, after everything he put her through? The frustration began to build in the weeks after his first return, like a sickening pressure behind her eyes, until one day it just exploded.

CHAPTER 14

SALLY WAS BRINGING David his breakfast when it happened. He was still in bed and she wanted to do something nice for him, to reach out and bridge the gap that had opened up between them. She'd made kippers, mushrooms, and fried tomatoes, with wholemeal toast and hot tea.

As she carried the steaming food up the old wooden stairs on a tray, Sally began to think about why she was reaching out to him and what had come between them. She wondered why she was always the one who tried to make peace and why David never met her halfway. She was the one who had to put up with him and look after him, the least he could do was let her in on what was going on.

By the time she got to the bedroom she was livid. Her arms were vibrating, and her anger was like a white hot light—its glare washed out every detail of the room. Without saying a word she lifted the tray and flung it at David's head.

Luckily, her aim was poor, and the kippers, the tea and the toast ended up all over the headboard and the bedroom wall.

"Why won't you talk to me about it?" Sally

shrieked. "Why? Why? Why?" She tore her throat, she was so angry.

David pulled the bed covers over his head. Sally stood there panting, unable to believe what she'd just done. After a minute or two David slipped out of bed, put on his slippers and dressing gown, and shuffled off to his study, where he stayed for the rest of the day.

Sally was actually quite scared by what she'd done. She'd never acted that way before. It shocked her out of her anger and frustration, and she cleaned up the mess in the bedroom. David came down for supper that night, and Sally made her peace with him. She was tired of fighting, and she missed his company.

Even still, the old distances began to creep back into their relationship. They spent less time together and weren't as intimate with each other. Neither of them wanted to bring up the subject of the Beast. Sally knew in her heart that it would return and take David away again. This imagined absence, or at least the anticipation of it, was almost as unbearable as losing David to the Beast.

The Beast did return some weeks later, and it was after David returned to her, on this occasion, that his attitude towards Sally changed. He became more conciliatory, sensing perhaps, the lengths to which he put her when he was gone.

This was when David came the closest to opening up.

CHAPTER 15

IT WAS A warm night, but they decided to light the fire anyway and make it an occasion with a good bottle of Merlot. Sally had cooked lamb shanks, and they were feeling nicely full and a little tipsy.

"I don't know what's up with this weather," she mused. "One minute it's pouring down, the next it's bright sunshine. It's been that way all week. Still it's good for the wildflowers in the forest. There'll be a carpet of them next week, I expect."

"It's different in the heart of the forest," David said. Then he paused, and a brief frown passed across his face. Sally and he had never gone into the heart of the forest, which covered nearly 4,000 hectares. They'd only explored the periphery.

Sally sensed an opportunity and reached out to him. "Is it much darker there? In the middle of the forest, I mean."

"It's more primal and untouched. Very few people have ever gone all the way into it, possibly a handful in living memory. There are parts of it that no human has ever seen."

Sally took a sip of her wine. She didn't want to pry too much, or she'd frighten him off the subject. It was like coaxing a wild animal out of its lair—she couldn't make any sudden or threatening moves.

"They've always been important to your family, haven't they?"

David turned to her, surprised at her perception and for a moment, she thought she might have scared him off, but he looked back into the fire and continued.

"My grandfather told me a lot about the woods. He was fascinated with them almost as if they were a part of him. He told me it was the same for many of my ancestors. There was one especially, a Laird of the Manor, back in the eighteenth century. They still talk about him in the town—Matthew McCavendish, he's the one I get the family curse from."

"The family curse?" Sally repressed a smile, she didn't want David to think she wasn't taking him seriously.

"My black moods, it's genetic, apparently. He was 'much given to black moods,' if you believe the local lore. He went to university in Edinburgh to study science and medicine, but his real interests were apparently far more occult. He got involved with some secret societies and then returned home under a cloud without completing his degree."

"Why?"

"He had some sort of breakdown, lots of rumours about it, all very melodramatic. There was gossip about him messing with dark forces—that sort of nonsense. That was the start of his mental health problems."

"Did he find the forest comforting, like we do?"

"He was fascinated with it. He even wrote a paper on the forest and published it privately. He mapped quite a lot of the territory and studied its flora and fauna. He proved there were species of plants in the forest that go back to prehistoric times, to the Paleozoic era even."

"Really?"

"Yes, that means it's pretty much untouched since before the Ice Age, before Britain was an island even."

"That's incredible. Why don't more people know about this? Why isn't the forest some sort of World Heritage Site?"

"Well, I'm afraid Matthew had some rather . . . erm . . . colourful views about the forest that don't sit well with the scientific establishment."

"Occult views you mean?"

David nodded. "Yes, he had a lot of strange ideas it seems. He was very influenced by an ancient set of beliefs called the Qu'rm Saddic heresy. Its believers have been persecuted since before Mesopotamian times."

"And what does this have to do with the forest?" said Sally with a touch of nonchalance, careful not to reveal how fascinated she was.

"He believed that the forest was one of the 'Quiet Places.'"

"Quiet Places?"

"It's all rather complicated. I'm not sure I understand it myself." David reached for the wine bottle and refilled their glasses. He stared into his glass for a while, as if the answer could be found in its rich blend of tannins. For one awful moment Sally thought he was going to leave it there, but he took a deep breath and continued.

"Apparently, there are older worlds than this one which came into existence before ours."

"I'm not sure I'm following you."

"Okay, let's call them higher planes then. You can follow that, right?"

"I guess."

"Okay, so these higher planes also contain life much older than ours, but not so corporeal."

"Like angels and demons, that sort of thing?"

"Erm . . . probably. Usually these beings can't . . . I guess you'd say manifest here in our world. But they can sometimes enter it through Quiet Places like the forest, and we can even leave this world if we want to, and if we know how."

"So these Quiet Places, they're like a portal or something?"

"More like a place where a portal can be opened. It's because they're very old. They haven't changed in eons, and they're the parts of our world that came into existence first, the bits that everything else grew from."

"Is that strictly scientific?"

"I don't think so. Matthew was more of a mystic than a scientist."

"And he put all this in his paper, that's where you read it, right?"

"Yes, but the paper doesn't cover all of it. He talks about it more in his journals."

"Wait, you've got his journals? They're here in the cottage. Can I see them?"

David furrowed his brow as if in pain. His head dropped to his chest and he hunched his shoulders as he went into himself. In her excitement, Sally had overreached herself and now she'd lost him. Her heart pounded as she thought of something to say.

"I need to get some more wood for the fire," David said finally, and he got up and made to leave.

"Wait, David, please," Sally said. "Come and sit down. The fire's okay, we don't need any more wood."

"I better get some more." He didn't even bother to look at her as he left the room.

"David . . . please . . ."

The closing of the back door was his only reply.

The next day, Sally saw that David had fitted a lock to his study door, excluding her from any further family secrets.

CHAPTER 16

TWO WEEKS AGO:

DAVID COULDN'T KEEP her out for long. It was after the third time the Beast took him that Sally read the pamphlet Jane had given her.

After the section on Hettie of the Hedgerow, Sally flipped forward in the pamphlet to the next chapter where she found the section on the 'Curse of the McCavendish family.' The chapter was on Phantom Black Dogs of the Highlands and the Gaelic mythological hound Cù-Sith in particular. It was the last section of this chapter that opened her eyes to the complicity of everyone who lived in Dunballan, including Jane. It was here that she learned something of the dark burden of David's family:

Perhaps the most unique variation on the legend of the Black Dog isn't actually a dog, but a giant black cat, of strange appearance, more commonly known as the Beast of Dunballan. Dunballan is one of the remotest and least visited towns in the Highlands.

It's also home to some of the strangest folklore of that area.

Possibly the strangest thing about the tale of the Beast is that the person at the centre of the myth, Matthew McCavendish—Laird of Dunballan—is a real historical figure and many of the events can be historically verified. Matthew was born to a wealthy and propertied family who once owned most of the lands around Dunballan.

From an early age Matthew showed great promise in his studies, reading Latin before the age of ten and quoting long passages of Shakespeare from memory. He went up to St Andrew's University when he was only sixteen years old, to study Classics, but had to return after only four terms due to 'incipient melancholy.' Matthew it seems was 'given to black moods,' and it's quite possible that he was too young and too homesick to cope with the pressures of academic life.

It wasn't until he was twenty years old that he would return to university, this time to Edinburgh to study medicine. The four years must have made all the difference, because to begin with, Matthew prospered in his studies. He graduated first in his class for the first two years and was invited to join many of Edinburgh's most eminent scientific societies. He moved in many acclaimed scientific circles, but Matthew also began to keep scandalous company, and that proved his downfall.

In those days it was very fashionable for young men of the upper classes, to join secret societies, or gentleman's clubs, such as the Hellfire Club in London and the Beggar's Benison in Edinburgh. The purpose of these societies was manifold, on the one hand they were hot-beds of 'free thought' and occult practices, on the other, they were an excuse for licentious and decadent behaviour.

Matthew soon graduated to the most secret and scandalous of all these societies—the infamous Faith Before Man. No one is certain exactly where its name came from, but there is documentary evidence that it was also known by the longer title: The Venerable Order of the Faith that Came Before Man. The society wasn't very big and was more interested in occult practices than the usual sex and debauchery these clubs indulged in. In this respect it probably had more in common with the later Hermetic Order of the Golden Dawn than the Beggar's Benison.

It seems that the magical beliefs of the Faith Before Man might have been influenced by their study of writings from antiquity. Their secret rites were certainly associated with heresy as this excerpt from the Edinburgh Evening Courant in 1738 shows:

"This foul calamity, it is believed, was precipitated by the group's close study of a most ancient set of scrolls, of a pagan nature, dating from before the birth of Christ and outlining beliefs and practices of a nature so diabolical that one Church Authority has claimed they would change the consciousness of every man and woman of Christendom should their message be proliferated."

The precise nature of the 'foul calamity' isn't known but, as far as we can ascertain, one of the society's magical rites must have gone extremely wrong, for a week later the Edinburgh Weekly Journal reported:

"The tide of public opinion has begun to turn against a number of the elite clubs that populate our city, following the scandal of the not-so-august gathering of moneyed rogues known as Faith Before Man. A recent exploit that involved dabbling in black arts saw one member dead and two leaving hold of their mental faculties. How long the upright and decent citizens of our fair city can tolerate such activity remains to be seen, but the society seems to have disbanded under a cloud, and not a moment too soon, in this publication's considered opinion."

Matthew's exact part in this scandal isn't known, but we do know he was subsequently expelled from the scientific societies he'd joined, and wasn't able to find work as a doctor when he graduated.

Matthew was saved from ruin and destitution by a surprise inheritance when his uncle unexpectedly died. He returned home to run the family estate but, despite his turn of fortune, he soon fell into one of the black moods to which he was prone. His old melancholy had returned, and he fell into a malaise that saw the decline of all his lands and property.

One morning, about a year after he moved back to Dunballan, Matthew's servants raised the alarm when he went missing from his mansion. A search party was formed in the town, and Matthew's lands were scoured. After two days of fruitless searching, the party finally came upon Matthew deep within the forests of his estate.

He was alive, but he was standing completely still, his eyes fixed on the distance, staring off into nothing at all. He didn't speak or acknowledge anything around him. Nothing anyone from the search party did or said could rouse him from this trance. He looked thin and feverish, having spent at least two nights exposed to the cold winds and the rain of a Highland winter.

Though he didn't respond to the men of the search party, Matthew hadn't lost the ability to walk, and they were able to lead him, still in a trance, out of the forest and back to his mansion. When, after a good few days, he had failed to rouse himself from this torpor, Matthew was transferred to a sanatorium. Though the staff at the sanatorium were able to keep him alive, they weren't able to improve his condition. As beds were scarce and Matthew needed no specialist care, they sent him home.

Within a week of returning home,

Matthew made a sudden and unexpected recovery. No one has been able to explain what happened to him or why he fell into a fugue state. The man himself was not at all helpful, refusing to discuss the matter with anyone, not even his doctor. He was not entirely cured, though, and would fall into the same waking stupor many more times, sometimes for days, sometimes for weeks at a time.

He left no heir when he died, so Matthew's mansion, and what was left of his estate, went to a younger cousin who moved his family into the grand house. Sadly, within months of taking up residence, the new owner came down with the same affliction that had troubled Matthew. All attempts to cure him of the condition were in vain and when he died, his son also developed the condition. Every successive heir has fallen prey to this same affliction, and this has given birth to the legend of the McCavendish family curse.

The McCavendish clan is a very private family and have not allowed the inherited condition to be studied, so we can only speculate on its origin. Some have suggested it's a genetic flaw that comes into effect in adulthood, but this doesn't explain why it only affects the oldest male heir or why the affliction only manifests when they inherit what's left of the estate.

While science has so far failed to explain the McCavendish family curse, local legend offers us an alternate explanation. It has long been rumoured that Matthew turned to the dark arts he learned in the Faith Before Man to rid himself of the terrible melancholy that plagued him. Deep in the heart of the forest bordering his estate, Matthew is said to have summoned a huge black Beast to rid him of his black moods.

Some versions of the legend cast the Beast as a denizen of Hell, others have it cross over from the lands of Faerie, but all of them agree that the creature feasted on the misery of men and women. Matthew most likely wanted it to consume his black moods so he could be done with them. The Beast, however, took far more than Matthew's sadness, it also took his soul.

In this respect, the Beast of Dunballan is not dissimilar to the legend of the Cù-Sith, the giant black dog of the Highlands, a harbinger of death who carries away the souls of the dead. Whereas the Cù-Sith is a psychopomp, a mythical figure who conveys the souls of the dead to the afterlife much like the Grim Reaper, the Beast of Dunballan didn't take Matthew's soul to the afterlife or, if it did, it didn't leave it there.

The Beast, it appeared, only borrowed Matthew's soul for short periods of time which was why he fell into a vegetative state. When the Beast returned his soul, he came back to himself. Quite a few of the servants who worked at the mansion have reported glimpsing the Beast in the grounds of the house, either before or just after one of Matthew's episodes. Sightings of the Beast in the forests around Dunballan continue to this day. Whatever hellish deal Matthew struck with the Beast, it seems it continues to haunt his family to this day, and according to legend, this is the true cause of the McCavendish family curse.

The curse, it appears, also extends to the townsfolk of Dunballan. Around the turn of the twentieth century, the present heir to the McCavendish estate, Hamish McCavendish, sold off most of the remaining lands and the mansion without moving in. He preferred to live in London and only kept a large cottage and a small parcel of land in Dunballan that he used for hunting holidays.

Roughly six months later, mass

hysteria broke out in Dunballan. Several of the townsfolk began to fall into a waking stupor similar to that suffered by the McCavendish family. Several of the womenfolk reported hearing from Hettie of the Hedgerow (see last chapter), who told them that the Beast of Dunballan was responsible for their misfortune. Hettie claimed they must either catch and kill the Beast or convince Hamish to return home. If the townsfolk speak of the Beast to an outsider, Hettie warned, it would mean their ruin. The folk of Dunballan have been a tight lipped bunch ever since (let's hope they don't mind me recounting this tale).

A hunt was organised, but the Beast could not be found, so word was sent to Hamish that he had to come home. Hamish dismissed the pleas at first, thinking them superstitious nonsense. More townsfolk fell to the curse, however, and couldn't be roused, so finally he relented. Things had not gone well for him in London. He'd lost most of his money in gambling debts and bad property deals.

Hamish returned home, and the townsfolk suffered no further misfortunes. From that day forth, there has always been at least one member of the McCavendish family living in Dunballan.

That's where that chapter ended. Sally couldn't believe what she'd just read. She'd picked up the pamphlet out of boredom and curiosity. She had no idea it would contain such a bombshell.

She stared at the badly printed text of the last page till it went out of focus. Sally was feeling too many emotions at once—rage, incomprehension, and betrayal, all so intense they almost cancelled each other out.

They knew.

That was what Sally couldn't take. Every person in Dunballan knew what David was going through and what Sally had to suffer because of it. That's why they could never hold Sally's eye when she met them. That's why they smiled and nodded and scurried away, clustering in little groups, gossiping amongst themselves.

They were all complicit in the same guilt. They'd known what was going to happen from the moment she and David arrived, and they approved of it. Not only approved of it, they needed her and David to go through it for their own selfish ends.

Jane knew what Sally was being put through, and she tried to make friends with her. Sally could hardly believe her gall. Then, when she couldn't be Sally's friend, Jane gave her this leaflet to rub her face in it. What was passed off as folklore by her uncle was actually happening. Sally and David were still living through it, all these years later.

That's why David had been called home, so these sinister little people could get their claws into him. That's why he asked Sally to come with him and why he was so nice to her at first, because he knew what he was going to have to face. What they were going to make him do.

Sally could forgive David, she loved him, but she hated Dunballan. She hated Dunballan, and she despised the Beast.

Then the dam of her emotions burst and the rage took over. The pamphlet slipped from her fingers and fell to the floor. Sally stood up and stamped on it, grinding her foot into the torn pages.

She kicked the pamphlet towards the far wall and the rusted staples came apart, sending pages skittering all over the living room.

Sally screamed and cursed the people of Dunballan. She kicked the furniture and threw pots at the wall, covering the floor in pottery shards. When her initial outburst was spent, her anger cooled and hardened, and a plan began to form in her mind.

That was when Sally decided she would find the voice, the one that spoke to her from the thicket, the one that the pamphlet also mentioned. This was magic that belonged to Sally. Hettie had chosen to speak to her and not anyone else. The pamphlet had shown Hettie helped those in extreme misery, like Sally. She would listen to this voice, she would learn from it.

Then she would take its magic and use it against Dunballan. She would kill the Beast and take back her man.

CHAPTER 17

SALLY HAD ONLY been this deep into the forest once before. That was yesterday. She'd had David with her then, or rather his mindless body.

Hettie had shown her the way that time. Whispering to her from the coppice, bending the undergrowth to point her in the right direction. She had to find her own way now, retracing the path from memory. That became harder the farther she got into the woods, especially as the sun was going down and evening was creeping in.

A rotting moss covered log blocked her way—she didn't recognise it. Had she taken a wrong turn? Sally looked around the forest for any landmarks she might recognise.

The silver birches were giving way to pines, which grew closer together, and the temperature in this part of the forest dropped. The cool air brought a sudden flash of lucidity. Sally thought about what she was doing here in the middle of the forest, and it suddenly seemed insane.

Was she really going to save David this way, or was she putting him in more danger? Would any of the ritual work? Could she really immobilise and kill the

Beast, or would it tear her to pieces? She was doing all of this because of a voice she heard in the underbrush, was she actually losing her mind?

She stumbled around the log and came to a thick coppice of saplings and shrub. As if in answer to her fears, it began to move as though a sudden gust was shaking it, even though she heard and felt no wind.

The tiny branches of the coppice rattled, the twigs beneath them skittered, and the many leaves moved in a flurry. The darkness at the heart of the shrubs seemed to throb, as the overlapping sounds of the thicket formed themselves into a voice.

"Do not fear—do not fear—do not fear little sister. You have no need—have no need—have no need for doubt."

As always happened in Hettie's presence, Sally felt her certainty return and her negative feelings, her fear, her anger and her pain ebb away, as if absorbed by Hettie herself. But not so much as usual. Sally still had a slim shred of doubt.

"What if I'm endangering David and myself? How do you know this will work on the Beast?"

"Have I ever steered you wrong—steered you wrong—steered you wrong?"

"I don't know, you've told me lots of things, but how do I know if any of them are true?"

"What about the journals—the journals—the journals, were they not where I told you—told you—told you?"

Sally felt the weight of the journals in the cloth bag on her shoulder. Hettie was right, she had told Sally exactly where to find the journals and what she would find in them. Sally could even remember the mood she was in as she went in search of them.

CHAPTER 18

SALLY FELT FURIOUS and betrayed, but she was also eaten up with curiosity. She'd been kept in the dark far too long—she needed some answers.

The last few months she'd been living through a situation that seemed ludicrous, impossible even, if you spent a few minutes thinking rationally about it. It was as though she'd fallen into some waking dream where all natural logic had been suspended.

Sally wasn't certain why she'd simply accepted everything and then learned to cope with it. The remoteness of Dunballan probably had a lot to do with it, as did the isolation she felt. Sally had no one with whom she could discuss what was happening. She had no friends in Dunballan and had lost touch with her friends in London. She hardly spoke to anyone in her family, and she doubted any of them would help even if she reached out to them.

There was only David, and David had closed himself off. He was too embarrassed by what he was going through and possibly a little guilty for having dragged Sally into it. In spite of how cross she was with him, Sally understood his predicament.

All the same, she had no perspective on what she

was going through, no one to examine it with and no way to put it into any context. Context was what she required and, to get context, she needed answers.

So, when Hettie mentioned Matthew's journals, Sally was eager to read them. Hettie even told her where she would find them—in David's study. If she was honest, Sally already knew that's where they were, but David's study was off-limits to her. It was his little haven, and she wasn't supposed to go in there, even to clean. She needed permission to hunt through it, and Hettie had given her that.

Sally collected the wooden-handled axe from the woodshed and marched upstairs with it. David's study had been locked since their little fireside chat when the journals had first come up. There was no need for him to do that, she'd always respected his privacy. The lock was a slap in the face. It was one exclusion too many. Sally had wanted to unlock David from the moment they first met. She would have to make do with his study.

Sally raised the axe above her head and brought it down so hard, she heard her shoulder click. The axe bit into the door with a satisfying thunk. The old, weathered oak splintered, but the door didn't give. She brought the axe down again and again, breaking into a sweat. The muscles in her upper arms and shoulders began to ache. Sally wished she was in better shape— this was harder than she'd thought.

Eventually she hacked all the way around the square, cast iron lock and kicked the door with a cry of anger and frustration. The lock remained where it was as the door swung open. David would be very angry when he saw what she'd done, but Sally didn't care. If he didn't want her to act this way, then he shouldn't have locked it in the first place.

David's study hadn't been dusted since they moved in, probably even longer. The room smelled of must, stale air and old books. David's desk was covered with mountainous piles of paper, and Sally couldn't see his laptop anywhere. The bookshelf looked like it was about to fall apart under the weight of all its books. The books spilled over in untidy piles, onto the floor, some as tall as Sally.

She had no idea where to start looking for the journals. She wasn't even certain what they looked like. All she knew was they'd be very old and hand written, not printed. Sally hunted through the bookshelf first, then the piles of books all over the floor, picking up the oldest books and flicking through them.

This got her nowhere, so she went through David's desk and, when that proved fruitless, she scoured every other corner of the study. At the bottom of an old cupboard, she came upon the chest. It looked like something pirates would bury on a deserted island. It was about three hundred years old and made of dark-stained wood. Most annoyingly, it was locked. Sally looked at the axe she'd left by the door and wondered if she could bring herself to destroy a venerable antique.

Luckily she didn't have to—there was a tarnished brass key lying on a shelf above the chest. Sally tried the key and opened the chest. It smelled of bitumen, fading leather and old musty paper. Inside she found fifteen journals all neatly stacked. They were leather bound with gilt edged pages.

She lifted them out and flicked through the pages. Matthew McCavendish's handwriting was precise but florid and took Sally a moment to decipher. When she'd got the hang of it and was able to scan each of the journals, she honed in on the volumes she wanted—those that contained entries about the Beast and its origins.

This wasn't an easy job, nor was it a quick one. The journals were written over a ten-year period and some of the entries went on for pages and pages. The room grew dim as the sun began to set, and Sally's stomach growled. She hadn't eaten since breakfast, but she didn't want to stop until she'd found everything she needed.

When she'd been through every journal, she retired to the living room with a small selection and a light supper. She didn't feel like feeding David—she was too angry—so she left him where he was in the conservatory.

The first journal she picked out covered the six months before Matthew McCavendish had to leave Edinburgh in shame and disgrace. It covered many details of his life that weren't relevant, but he wrote a lot about being a member of various gentlemen's clubs and societies, including Faith Before Man.

As far as Sally could tell, most of the societies Matthew joined were an excuse for members to get drunk and hire prostitutes, although it all seemed a bit homoerotic as they mainly masturbated one another while looking at naked women. There was some talk of 'radical politics'—or what would have been considered 'radical' at the time—and even the odd mention of pagan beliefs, but this didn't seem to be the main purpose of the gatherings. It was just one more illicit thrill. It all seemed a bit strange and seedy to Sally, and nothing like she'd imagined these blasphemous societies to be.

Only the Faith Before Man seemed to have any interest in actual esoteric beliefs. As far as Sally could tell, it was an elite society that was secret even to other societies and operated entirely in the shadows. Its members were devoted to uncovering certain occult philosophies that had been lost to the ages. They mainly did this by poring over a cache of ancient and forbidden texts that the members acquired for great sums. They were particularly interested in an ancient set of beliefs called the Qu'rm Saddic Heresy, or The Faith that Came Before Man, which is where they might have gotten their name.

There was one passage that Matthew wrote, towards the end of a later journal, that really gripped Sally's attention:

June 21st ____

It has been three nights now and I have barely slept. The laudanum does nothing for me. I can neither hold back nor suppress the memories of that night. I close my eyes and the images rear up in my mind, in more terrible detail than when I first beheld them. They will not let me rest.

I am a dishevelled wreck of raw nerves and wild fancy. I start at the slightest sound from the street. I have shut-up the windows and closed the shutters, but the cacophony of the city finds me still. I have no appetite and even less wish to leave my rooms in search of food. I'm too distracted to read, and yet I have nothing else to take my mind off the events of that night. I cannot go in search of human company for I fear I am tainted, that my peers will read in my countenance some of what has come to pass, and will know the deeds to which I've stooped.

So I turn instead to my journal. I have neglected it of late, but now it is my one, slim comfort. I had such high hopes for it when I began. Was it really only two years ago that I wrote in these very pages, of my ambition to chronicle my ascendancy into the loftier realms of science and my transcendence through the secrets of the occult? I had hoped to develop a new system of thought in which both could be synthesised to the benefit of the other. Now I fear that ambition must be abandoned. My sole hope is that, by setting down what happened, by capturing every memory that hounds me relentlessly, I can exorcise myself of them. While every word that was uttered is as clear to me now as when I first heard it, and every sight I beheld, or purported to behold, is carved like a stone relief onto my mind, I will endeavour to put it all down in these pages. I know there is little chance that this will relieve me of their burden, but I have no other options—this journal is my last resort.

My pen shakes as I try to gather my thoughts. I am procrastinating, I know. I am trying to postpone re-living these events by putting them down in words. I know this is foolish, and I must stop wasting time. Let me try a little laudanum and I will endeavour to continue . . .

Even in Edinburgh, with its arctic winter nights that barely improve in the summer, the temperature was cold for the time of year. I arrived at Patterson's residence in Hanover Street a little later than I would have liked, but I had other matters to attend to first.

I was greeted by Moran, Patterson's manservant, a slovenly and unkempt man for whom I do not care. He showed me, unannounced, into the drawing room, the largest space in Patterson's residence. The spacious, high ceilinged room had been stripped of all its furniture and furnishings. All that remained were the drawn curtains and bare floorboards. I entered to find McKendrick and Patterson eagerly awaiting me.

"What's this," I said. "Are the others not here yet? What of Stevenson, McGregor, and Smythe?"

"I didn't tell them about our gathering," Patterson said. He was wearing only an unwashed shirt and a pair of breeches. He patently hadn't shaved that morning and his thinning blonde hair was plastered to his forehead with sweat. "We need a much smaller group for our first foray."

"To be honest," said McKendrick, who was leaning up against the mantelpiece, "I'm not sorry to be rid of Smythe, or her insistence that we pay homage to an interminable litany of goddesses, before we can begin any ritual."

McKendrick was quick to disparage Smythe and her pagan beliefs, but he was happy to accept her patronage and the wealth she lavished on our society. He was as immaculately dressed as ever in a short double breasted waistcoat and knee breeches, all perfectly tailored to his tall, broad frame. He had also trimmed his large, military moustache since I last saw him. I looked around the room for the robes and artefacts Patterson had chosen for our ceremony but could see none.

"Are we to draw a pentacle on the floor?" I asked. "Or did you have some other symbol in mind?"

"Actually, I wasn't intending to use any symbols in the ceremony," Patterson replied.

"None at all?"

Patterson shook his head. "Nor any wands, swords or other paraphernalia."

"The d_____d fool doesn't even want to invoke the Four Watchtowers," McKendrick said.

"But without the Guardians of the Watchtowers, how will we open the way?" I said. "How will we call upon the elements for protection?"

"We won't need to," Patterson assured us. "The Rite of Adocentyn isn't that sort of ceremony. It's from a tradition that's much older than any of the Hermetic arts."

"So how did you find out about it then?" barked McKendrick. "Turned up some new scroll from your Uncle's collection?"

Patterson's late Uncle, as I think I've mentioned before in these pages, had been an avid collector of ancient and forbidden manuscripts. These included original copies of the Corpus Hermeticum and the Picatrix, in both Greek and Arabic. When he passed away, he left his entire collection to Patterson. The rarest and most precious items from this collection had led to the formation of our society, and also helped christen it.

Through means we had never discovered, Patterson's Uncle had procured perhaps the only surviving copies of the Codex Transfiguratio, the Codex Conscientia, and the Vos Hokkumah Scrolls. Among the most forbidden and blasphemous texts in the history of civilisation, this collection of writings comprised the only known repository of the heretical Qu'rm Saddic teachings, also known, in times of yore, as The Faith that Came Before Man. Each one of them had been copied by hand and translated into Anglo Saxon from tongues so ancient that no record of them yet remains.

"It was a game my Uncle used to play with me that provided the inspiration," said Patterson.

"Parlour games, you want us to find the Gate with parlour games?" McKendrick said with great derision.

"Not parlour games. I think my Uncle was secretly trying to train me to do the rite. He'd take my brother and me into a bare room, like this one, and he'd ask us where we'd like to visit. We could go anywhere in the world. We'd choose a place and he'd take us there with the power of his words. He'd start by describing the scene, and then he'd walk around the space and begin to point out certain details to us. After a while he'd get us to join in with him, and we'd start to point out what we saw and describe our surroundings, too. Eventually, matters would come to a point where we wouldn't need to describe things to each other in order for us all to see them. It became akin to a shared hallucination. What's more, we could even verify this later."

"Verify it, how?" demanded McKendrick.

"When I was a child I was obsessed with the port at Alexandria. I'd read about it in my father's library, and I'd even written poems about it and drawn pictures of what I thought it looked like."

"I'll wager they were no better than the doggerel and daubings you produce now."

McKendrick was constantly deriding Patterson's work. He cared neither for the paintings nor the poetry Patterson produced.

Patterson ignored his barb and continued. "So, naturally, one of the first places that I chose to explore in the game was the Alexandrian port. I spent hours exploring it with my brother and Uncle. We went everywhere, including a little stone archway for taking livestock into the city. The keystone on the archway had a very specific stonemason's symbol. My brother spotted it first and then he pointed it out to my Uncle and me. Years later as a young man, I visited Alexandria by boat and spent several nights in the port. I was gripped with a sense of déjà vu. It all looked familiar, as if I had visited before, even though it was my first time there. Then I remembered the game I had played with my Uncle and realised that everything was just as I had seen as a boy. It was as though I had been transported to the very spot where I now stood. I made a point of searching out the stone arch, and it was right where we'd seen it in the game, with the same symbol on the keystone. We'd never been to Alexandria when we played the game, yet we'd seen a unique landmark that, years later, I could independently verify."

"Well, that's all very fascinating," I said.

"But what does any of this have to do with the rite of Adocentyn?"

"It says, in the third tractate of the Vos Hokkumah Scrolls, that to enter the city of Adocentyn one must think with the mind of God and see with the eyes of God."

"We've all read the blasted scrolls," said McKendrick.

"I know, it was me that showed them to you. So you'll also know that in the Codex Transfiguratio it says: 'the imagination is the Queen of all the senses, for she is closest to the thoughts of God.' Imagination is the key to all magic, you know it is. Every occult ritual and symbol is merely a way of focusing the imagination so we can recreate reality just as God once created it."

"You're not convincing me."

"In the beginning was the 'word' and the 'word' was with God. He is the ultimate storyteller, trapped within His own story. What better way to escape His story than with another story? The Rite of Adocentyn is a collectively shared story in which we're all storytellers. We counter the prison of Creation with a story of our own. That's how we enter Adocentyn, and that's where we'll find the Gate."

Nothing in life had seemed the same to me. No part of my existence or any others, had remained untouched since I encountered this central truth of the Qu'rm Saddic Heresy. The pen still shakes in my hand as I recall each appalling revelation that confronted me while I poured over Patterson's scrolls by candlelight. Written in Anglo-Saxon, the language of the Frisian settlers who, in Roman times, first brought these teachings to our shores and, at the same time, gave birth to the myth of Joseph of Arimathea and his sacred repository of teachings.

Many times I looked up from the parchment to see Patterson's grave countenance examining me, directing my attention to new passages that shook me to my very core and destroyed every certainty to which I had ever cleaved. Every ounce of my reason rose up in opposition to this one core truth, but my heart bade me believe it.

God is not just the breath of life that animates all living things. He is also a prisoner in His own creation. Just as a heavy cloud falls to earth as a thousand different drops of rain, God has entered the material world as a million different consciousnesses, each one perceiving itself as an individual entity. For this reason, we never realise our collective divinity, never see the material world for the jail it truly is, and this ignorance is the greatest form of tyranny. Even Heaven is a part of this snare, for it is but a way-station, a temporary respite from our journey back to becoming one with the source of Creation from which we once came and of which we were always a part.

We are not without means of escape, though. However slim they are, there are stresses built into the architecture of the universe, tiny nooks and crannies through which our souls can slip and attain their true divinity. The scrolls had taught us such a Gate could be accessed within the mythical city of Adocentyn in ancient Egypt. Adocentyn can no longer be found on Earth. It exists on a higher plane now, within an older world than ours.

I had first read of Adocentyn, the legendary city built by the thrice-great Hermes Trismegistus, in the Picatrix, that Arabian treatise on talismanic magic of which Marsilio Ficino, the Renaissance scholar who translated the Corpus Hermeticum, was so fond. Our study of Patterson's forbidden texts had taught us that the account of the city of Adocentyn in the Picatrix had a much older source. The Codex Transfiguratio described a rite that would allow the intrepid to access the ancient city and, once there, to search out the Gate.

Since discovering this, our elite society had become obsessed with deciphering the maddening clues within the text in order to enact the Rite. Now, it seemed, Patterson's Uncle might have known how to conduct the Rite all along and, furthermore, secretly trained his nephew without Patterson ever realising.

I could see, by the expression on McKendrick's face, that he was not unmoved by Patterson's argument. McKendrick fancied himself a hard-headed pragmatist. A botanist by training, I knew that he supplemented his scientific studies with occult study and not, as he claimed, out of a conviction that 'there was more to creation than can be found on a dissecting table.' Rather, I considered him a thrill seeker and, what may be worse, a man with a terrible will to power.

His family was very well connected in

the political world, and there was a seat in some rotten borough waiting for him as soon as he tired of his studies. McKendrick told me once, that he believed true power, the purest kind of power over other men, was not found in the ballot box, but in the occult. His older brother, now a junior minister, had been an explorer when he was younger. He came back from Africa with stories of the Babalawo, Yoruba high priests who worship the Orishas, and hold incredible sway over their followers. When McKendrick spoke of this power, his eyes came alive with a lust I found unnatural. To see him seduced by Patterson's logic swayed me also, I must confess.

Had I but the prescience to cry 'desist' at that moment, to persuade us all to let go of such folly and bend our efforts to another end, we might have been spared the terror that was to follow. But sadly, I lacked such essential precognition, and our dreadful tragedy played itself out to a most bitter end.

"So, how do we go about commencing this rite of yours?" McKendrick asked, addressing Patterson with a newfound regard.

"We need to take ourselves out of this space, and into another. For a start, gentlemen, I suggest you remove your coats. The sun is merciless at this time of day in the east of Egypt."

The fire in the grate had fallen to embers, and the room was large and given to draughts. Nonetheless, I took off my topcoat and within minutes, I forgot the loss of it, as Patterson described our journey across the hot sands of Egypt in the most vivid detail.

"Up ahead of us, on the crest of that hill," Patterson continued. "Do you see it? A wall, fully twelve miles long. That, my friends, marks the perimeter of Adocentyn. Tell me how it looks to you."

I looked up to where Patterson was pointing. In my mind's eye the image was becoming clearer. I pictured an ancient wall but not much else. As we drew closer I began to imagine more detail, then, as if he was describing the very thing I was picturing, McKendrick said: "It's built in the style of the Early Dynastic Period, only it looks far more sophisticated, both in terms of its design and construction. The stones are so white they fairly seem to glow as the sun's rays hit them."

We trudged on up the hill, describing to one another how the sand spilled into our shoes and the heat beat mercilessly down. I actually felt sweat break out on the back of my neck. As we reached the crest of the hill, we stood still and looked at each other in surprise.

"It's like an oasis," said McKendrick. "There's lush, fertile grass growing all around."

"And look," I said. "There's a lagoon, just ahead of us. The water is so blue. See how it fairly sparkles in the sun?"

"Do you see the fish leaping?" said Patterson. "A fisherman would never go hungry here."

We walked around the lagoon and approached the city wall which reared up ahead of us.

"Look, there's an entrance," I cried, pointing to a large opening in the wall. "And look at that relief above it, it's so meticulously carved."

"It depicts an Ibis," said McKendrick. Though I'd given him no clue, that's exactly what I also saw carved into the rock above the entrance.

"It seems to move," said Patterson. "To be watching us."

"That's an illusion," said McKendrick. "It's just the heat haze from the sun affecting the shadows."

"That's one explanation, but I suspect there are other forces at play."

Whatever the reason, we all saw the relief move, as if the Ibis was turning its head, with its long beak, to observe us. Though my body was still in Hanover Street, I no longer saw the empty walls and bare floors of Patterson's drawing room. I was wholly in Egypt, standing at the entrance to the city of Adocentyn.

Patterson knelt and bade us do the same. He put his hands together as if in prayer and intoned: "Guardians of the Castle, Lord Bull, Lord Eagle, Lord Hound, and Lord Lion, we humbly request your permission to enter Adocentyn and conduct ourselves without harm."

In brief succession we all heard a bull bellow, an eagle cry, a hound howl, and a lion roar. Each noise sounded incredibly near and yet seemed to issue from the depths of the city. There was something otherworldly in the echoing quality of each call.

Patterson stood. "I think we have permission to enter."

I will not exhaust myself by recording

the many marvels we witnessed in Adocentyn. Suffice to say we saw a multitude of images and symbols graven onto the walls of the ancient buildings. In the wide open plazas there were many huge trees, all bearing multiple types of fruits. We continued to describe all of this to one another, stopping occasionally to marvel at one of the many stone or metal statues that populated the city. It was as if our words, and our shared perceptions of them, intensified every sight we beheld.

Not once did we see a single inhabitant. The whole city was deserted and looked as if it had been that way for countless eons. Presently, we came to a castle in the centre of the city.

"See here," said Patterson. "It is just as the Picatrix described it. There are the four gates, aligned to the cardinal points of the compass, and above them are the guardians who granted our entry, the Bull, the Eagle, the Hound, and the Lion."

Huge stone statues of the beasts sat atop each of the gates, looking at once more real than life, but also of another world entirely.

"And there's the tower," said McKendrick, pointing to the summit of the castle. "I'm no expert on the matter of ancient measurements, but I'll wager that's a full thirty cubits, and it has a rotunda on the top, just as we were expecting."

The rotunda atop the tower was glowing with an eerie light that changed from purple to deep blue as we beheld it.

We entered the tower by the western gate, beneath the Bull, and made our way directly to the base of the tower. There were only two doors in the whole of the base.

"One of these leads to the vaults, the other to the summit of the tower," said Patterson.

"Which do we choose?" I asked.

"Whichever one leads us to the Gate," said McKendrick.

"But which is that?"

"The third tractate of the Vos Hokkumah scrolls instructs us to think with the 'mind of God,'" said Patterson. "The Codex Conscienta tells us that God descended to the material plane in order to achieve the ultimate ascendance."

"We choose the vaults then?" said McKendrick.

"We choose the vaults," I said, with unexpected certainty.

The steps down to the vaults were on a steep spiral. Even though in reality, we were doing nothing more than walking around in a circle in Patterson's drawing room. We were so immersed in our mutually induced hallucination that we squinted in the waning light and wrinkled our noses at the dank odours that rose to greet us.

The stairs gave out on a long stone

passageway that led to a low ceilinged stone chamber. As we approached, the chamber seemed to glow with an unnatural light. When we entered we saw the glow came from a mosaic of the moon, set into the floor of the chamber. What was causing the mosaic to glow with such a sinister luminosity I cannot say, but it drew Patterson, McKendrick, and me towards it, as if we were moths drawn by a candle flame.

As we set foot upon the mosaic, a vision appeared before us.

We saw a maiden arrayed in a shining silver robe. Her skin was most delicate and pale, and her whole aspect denoted grace and an unmistakable devoutness. She smiled at us with the delicate humility of one who is quite perfectly chaste. I found myself filled with awe and gratitude, that such an immaculate, apotheosis of divine femininity should bestow her attention upon us.

"It's Monanom," said Patterson. "The dual goddess of the moon."

"And what would you travellers, so far from your homes, want within my chamber?" Monanom asked.

"We seek the Gate," said McKendrick.

"The Gate?"

"Yes, the Gate that leads out of Creation and frees us from the prison of this world."

"That Gate is not to be found in my chamber, or even this city."

"Blessed Monanom," Patterson said. "It is written that the way to the Gate is to be found within this city, and, we believe, also within your chamber."

"So you would find this Gate, would you?" said Monanom. "Think carefully before you answer."

"Of course we would find this Gate," said McKendrick. "Why else would we travel all this way?"

"And this is the wish of you all, is it?"

"It is," said Patterson.

Though I was reluctant to agree with my companions—for I knew in my heart it would grieve Monanom, and I could think of nothing worse than saddening her—I too said, "It is."

At that, the goddess bowed her head, and folded her robes around her, and then spun round with a sudden velocity. The temperature of the chamber plummeted, and we saw the reverse side of Monanom—the most hideous and repugnant crone I have ever laid eyes upon. I had forgotten that the dual sides of her nature sit back-to-back on the same body. The crone's breathing was hoarse, and came in long, slow bursts. A stream of saliva spilled from her near-toothless mouth, and a deep chuckle broke ominously from her throat.

"Are you sure you don't want to turn back?" she said.

"No, we want to press on," Patterson

said, though I could see he felt as apprehensive as I did.

A tremor shook the ground at our feet and the mosaic rose six inches out of the floor as though it were mounted on the head of a short column. All three of us fought to keep our footing.

"How about now, any second thoughts?" said the Crone.

"No," I said, though I hardly knew where the tenacity came from.

With that, the ceiling of the chamber collapsed and great chunks of masonry rained down all around us. It was a wonder that none of us were hit. The column beneath the mosaic rose up, with great speed, pushing through the hole in the ceiling and into the lower floors of the castle above us. We fell to our hands and knees to keep from falling off the mosaic.

"Now will you turn back?" cackled the Crone, a malevolent smile creasing her lined face as she rose too, hovering in the air above us.

"No, God d__n you," McKendrick shouted.

The column rose again, and the ceiling above us fell in, and then the ceiling above that and every ceiling above us, until the column had pushed through them all and we were out in the open, level with the rotunda on the tower.

The crone circled us in the air. "Now will you turn back?" she said.

"No," I gasped, but my arms and legs were shaking.

"Hold firm," Patterson told us. "She's trying to break our resolve. To keep us imprisoned forever in the material world."

The column rose higher, at greater speed, taking us so far from the ground that first the castle, then the whole of Adocentyn disappeared from view. I became afraid to glance over the edge of the growing column. I pulled my knees up against my chest until I was curled into a ball, and dug my fingers into the mosaic's tiles, turning my knuckles white with the effort. The others did much the same.

The Crone flew all around us, taunting us with her presence.

"Wouldn't you like to turn back now?" she called out.

None of us could muster speech, so we just shook our heads.

The column continued its ascent, but a fearful rumble passed through it. The outer edges of the column were starting to crack and fall away. The circumference of the mosaic, on which we crouched, got smaller and smaller, the column got thinner and thinner and we were all forced to our feet.

What was left of the column broke through the clouds and carried on rising. The column was now so thin that all three of us were standing pressed up against each other with our arms around one another's waists. The heels of our boots were hanging over the edge of what was left of the column. If one of us were to list even slightly to one side, he would have taken the others with him, plummeting into the vast expanse below.

We were now higher than the tallest mountain on the planet. The air at this height was too thin, and we were all having difficulty breathing. Stripped to our shirt sleeves, because of the heat of Egypt, we were now numb with exposure. The column crumbled so much that, eventually, there was only room for us to place a single foot each upon it, and attempt to balance precariously.

The Crone swooped around us, her black robe flapping like the wings of some giant bat. "Do you want to turn back?" she shrieked.

God forgive me, I did want to turn back. I wanted to be out of this predicament and away from this trial. I had lost my resolve. I had failed the test and wanted nothing more than for it to end. I could see the same sentiment on the faces of the two men to whom I clung.

However, some indefatigable core at the centre of our beings refused to let us give voice to our failure. We closed our eyes and trusted to our fortitude instead.

The column continued to climb and crumble at the same time. Finally we felt it fall away completely and there was nothing holding us at so great a height. My heart lurched, and ice cold terror seized my innards. I felt something inside myself simply snap and give way. I surrendered myself to it utterly, expecting at any moment to plummet to my death.

Instead of panic, I felt transcendence flood through me. Instead of falling, I found myself to be weightless. I opened my eyes and saw that I had been transported to another realm altogether, along with Patterson and McKendrick. We had come through our trial and we had succeeded. Whether we were in our astral bodies or simply our incarnate souls, I couldn't say. We were experiencing a type of existence and a form of perception that we had never been aware of before. I could see and even feel whole new spectrums of colour and entire new modes of thought and movement.

Away in the distance, I saw two pillars of what seemed to be frozen fire, burning with a fire's intensity, but not dancing like a flame. The pillars had been carved into ornate posts, and between the posts was a lattice work of what I can only describe as 'hard light' that glowed with an almost unbearable intensity.

Patterson gasped. "It's the Gate, we've found the Gate!" We were on the very edge of Creation, and we had found the way out. All things were easier and simpler on this plane and we only had to look at the Gate and wish to be near it for us to move towards it.

As we got closer, we found the Gate to be resonating at some impossible frequency that we could apprehend only in the core of our being. It suggested to us that the Gate was a sentient being, capable of unimaginable thoughts.

Not one of us had the least idea what to do at that point. We had found the Gate as we had planned, but that was as far as our plans extended. Beyond that we hadn't the least clue how to proceed. None of us were certain if we had courage enough to take the final plunge and attempt to go through the Gate. To leave behind all of Creation and be utterly unmade so as to free the God within ourselves.

The Gate itself appeared to have some sort of gravitational pull. The closer we got to it, the more it seemed to draw us in, as though we were boats on an incoming tide. It remained closed for the whole of our approach and, I must confess, the thought of opening it terrified me. I had no idea what would happen if it were to swing wide. What might lie beyond it, or what would happen to all that lay before it on this side.

I had even less of an idea how one would go about opening the Gate. What sort of key would unlock it? More importantly, what key would lock it again—and keep it locked—if it were to swing too wide?

As we were silently deliberating, floating ever closer to the Gate, I heard McKendrick gasp. He was looking off into the distance. At first I did not see what caught his attention. Then it became apparent. A small crowd of what I can only describe as entities was moving in our direction.

It is here that my powers of description fail me. I cannot adequately convey quite how these beings looked. They each appeared to be an intricate conglomerate of geometric shapes that were constantly folding and unfolding themselves into dimensions of space beyond my ability to perceive. They were golden in colour, but their surface seemed harder than any metal in existence and yet also more fluid than any liquid I've known. The sharp, angularity of their surfaces were reflecting what seemed to be an ever changing array of objects: one moment it was a multitude of eyes from creatures I doubt have ever existed, the next it was stars from no known cosmos, and in another moment, some black unfathomable gulf from the edge of time itself.

It was Patterson who recognised them for what they were.

"Archons," he cried. "Run, for God's sake run, we mustn't let them get near us!" I knew instantly why he was so alarmed. We had all read of the Archons. They are mentioned not only in the Vos Hukkumah Scrolls but also in the few remaining

Gnostic texts that are passed between collectors of rare manuscripts.

They are Lords of the outer realms of Creation, who patrol the very outskirts of existence. Their sole aim is to maintain the integrity of the material world and to keep every soul imprisoned within it forever. They are Creation's last line of defence against the enlightened and the liberated.

They are also terrifying and hideous beings, capable of tearing apart and devouring a living soul for an agonising eternity. That is why, in spite of the ineffable pull of the Gate, Patterson and I turned away from it and willed ourselves to move as fast as we could in the opposite direction.

McKendrick was a different matter, though. He remained where he was, as if transfixed by the sight of the Archons.

"Magnificent," he said, as the Archons bore down on us. "Such power, such incredible, undeniable power."

We called out to McKendrick as we fled. We begged him to join us, to get away while there was still time, but if he even heard our words, he did not heed them. He held up his arms in welcome to the Archons, mindful only of his overweening lust for power. The near unstoppable, crushing power that the Archons represented had mesmerised him and that, as I always suspected, was his unmaking.

The Archons fell on him.

I cannot describe the agony of his screams, or the psychic emanations his suffering gave off. Patterson and I felt them most acutely though, in the very depths of our being. Even now my eyes fill with tears as I try to write this. My pen falters and my stomach rebels. I am going to have to set aside this journal, so I may vomit. I am sorry to be so coarse, but it is the truth . . .

I am back, for there is one further thing

that I need to get down. The one thing that has haunted me more than any other part of the whole, lamentable experience.

As the Archons fell on McKendrick, a thick black mist sprang up beneath him, and swirled about his legs. It had the appearance of ink dropped into a glass of water, forming itself into viscous tendrils that ended in what appeared to be a cross between an infernal blossom and a tiny gaping mouth. As McKendrick screamed (dear God, let me forget those screams), the tendrils seemed to thicken and swell, as though they were glutting themselves, feasting on his terror and pain.

Patterson and I could bear no more of McKendrick's tortuous ordeal, and we fled as fast as we could, though we had no idea where we were going. Our own panic and terror grew with each passing second, and this drew more of the black mist to us, swirling around us as we tried to escape. It would seem that the mist and its tendrils was some kind of fauna, unique to this plane of existence.

The mist grew many black tendrils, and many blossom-like mouths, that I could neither outrun, nor outmanoeuvre, no matter how hard I tried. They latched on to me and began to feed on my misery and terror. It was the strangest sensation, not unlike being bled by leeches to release the bad humour. In a short while I started to feel nothing. All the pain and fear that had gripped me was siphoned off and I was released of it. It was not a transcendent or a joyful feeling, but it was not wholly unpleasant.

In a little while I blacked out.

When I came to, I was lying on the floor of Patterson's drawing room, in a pool of blood. At some point in all the confusion, I must have fallen and dashed my forehead on the corner of the mantelpiece. Being a head wound, there was a lot of blood, but it wasn't that serious, requiring six stitches that I later applied to myself. Patterson and McKendrick were not so unscathed.

I found Patterson a little while later, curled up in a foetal position beneath a bed in one of the guest rooms. He must have crawled there when he came to. He was quite traumatised by his experience and had lost the power of speech when I found him. I helped him out from under the bed, but all he could do was whimper whenever I addressed him, preferring to curl up in a chair with a blanket over his head.

McKendrick fared even worse. He was in the drawing room when I regained consciousness. He was still on his feet, staring vacantly in front of him, oblivious to all stimuli. He was in a totally vegetative state. He was breathing and was capable of movement, but he had been stripped of any intelligence or cognitive ability. More than that, he was quite patently lacking a soul. I had witnessed what had happened to that essential and immortal part of his being, and I still shudder when I consider its fate. What was left behind on this material plane was a hollow shell. A mockery of a human being, that brought only pity and loathing to all who looked upon it. A lamentable travesty stood in the place of the man he once was.

Moran was nowhere to be found, whether he had fled in the night, or what became of him, I know not. He has not been seen since by anyone of my acquaintance. I summoned what help I could and made sure that my friends were in good hands and receiving the best help available. Then I retired to my own quarters to tend to my wounds. I have not left since, except to acquire laudanum and food.

This is all I have the strength to write. I have nothing more to say about the ordeal. All I have thought about since is the strange black mist I encountered that, for all its demonic qualities, may well have saved my sanity.

That and the Gate itself. I cannot stop myself from wondering what the consequences might be should it ever be thrown open, and how that might be prevented. What would one use as a lock, and what would be the key for such an ethereal portal?

CHAPTER 19

SALLY LOOKED UP from the journal. Her eyes were tired from staring at so much closely written handwriting, and her back ached from being curled up in the same position too long.

She had been reading the journal for hours without a break. The fire in the grate was nothing but embers. She stretched her legs and back, and blinked her eyes. Everything in the room looked suddenly strange and unreal. She'd been so engrossed in Matthew's account of his out-of-body experience, it was as if she was there with him. Putting down the journal and coming back to earth was disconcerting. It took her a moment to readjust.

If she'd read the journal before coming to Dunballan, Sally would have considered it either pure fantasy or deluded ravings, but after everything she'd seen, she was more inclined to believe it. It certainly answered a lot of her questions, but it threw up just as many. The current volume was the last of the journals, but there were a few more entries. Perhaps the answers she needed could be found there.

Sally got up from the sofa—her throat was dry, and she really needed the toilet. She went to the bathroom, and then fixed herself a cup of peppermint tea and settled down to read the last of the entries. They became more sporadic and self-pitying as Matthew's life took a turn for the worse. He was expelled from the university and asked to leave all the societies he'd joined. His friends turned their backs on him, and he couldn't find any work.

McKendrick never recovered from the state they found him in. He died a few months later at his family home. Patterson had a mental breakdown, and then made a full confession of everything that happened to his doctor. The Doctor didn't seem to have any scruples about telling others what he'd learned, and the story soon spread. More stories came to light about the Faith Before Man, creating a scandal that exposed and disgraced all its members.

The one bit of good news Matthew had was the surprise inheritance of his uncle's estate, but this wasn't quite the reversal of fortune that he'd hoped. His uncle had left him a lot of debt, and Matthew didn't seem to be any better at running the estate. His problems only increased, and Matthew fell into a deep depression. The gaps between entries got longer and longer, and he complained more and more about all the time he lost to his debilitating moods.

The only thing that seemed to lift his spirits was finding a certain specialist bookseller. Matthew had continued to collect rare books on the occult, and he was always looking for book shops to sell the paper he wrote on the ancient forest. This bookseller not only took several copies of his paper, he also sold Matthew a unique grimoire by an unknown author. The grimoire fascinated Matthew, and he made notes on it in his journal.

Sally couldn't understand much of what he wrote, but she found one entry, towards the end of the journal, very interesting:

November 21st ___

Success! Sweet and blessed success. Finally I have the vindication I long sought. My heart is so light I believe I could burst out into song, were it not for my awful voice and the shocked dismay of the servants, who already think my habits queer enough.

I have lost several days to poring over the Grimoire, a dense and obscure text to be sure, but not an unrewarding one, given careful study. Though I know nothing about the author's character, or any detail of his life, he could perhaps have been a brother of mine (or even a sister?), so closely aligned are our thoughts and ambitions. Today I chanced upon a bestiary of sorts, a brief summary of an older text wherein the unnamed author attempted to categorise the many different inhabitants of the unseen and rarely glimpsed worlds. In amongst the references to the Heolfor, the Byrgen-Beorden and the many other beings whose existence I have already read of, he mentions the little-known Bréostwylmas.

Ulthar of Thoone, an Anglo-Saxon monk from the ninth century, was said to have conjured up these entities, though they inhabit not this world, but a higher realm. They appeared to him as a viscous, black mist with many mouths on the end of tendrils. He claimed to have witnessed them feeding off the negative emotions of lower life forms, draining them of their pain, their fear and their misery, which were like so much meat and drink to them.

These are the beings we encountered when we found the gate! Imagine my excitement to discover I am not the only one to have seen them and kept his sanity. The grimoire also contains an account of the ritual that Ulthar performed to summon the Bréostwylmas. It is complex, and most difficult to decipher, but I think I am up to it.

I recall, to this day, the blessed oblivion the Bréostwylmas brought when they drained me of my panic and terror. I think with longing of the release they might bring from the wretched melancholy that has plagued me ever since. A worse jailer than the Archons, it has robbed me of weeks and months, keeping me paralysed and a prisoner in my own bed. How free of it I could be if I were to offer it up to the Bréostwylmas as a feast. Let them suck the very sadness from the marrow of my bones and bleed me of this bitter, bitter humour.

I have one advantage that Ulthar had not—the forest. As one of the few 'Quiet Places' left in this world, it will be easier for me to open a portal for the Bréostwylmas to come through. My only concern is for the Gate. I will be exposing this world to its indefatigable pull. What effect might that have? What would happen to all the living souls nearby if it should swing wide? What is the key that would lock it? What? What? What?

There were only a few entries after this. They were hard to make out. Matthew's handwriting got smaller and harder to read, and much of what he said didn't make any sense. It seemed to Sally that Matthew was more intent on hiding something from whoever read the journal, than unburdening himself. The final entry of all was perhaps the most enigmatic.

I know! Oh dear Lord, I know . . . Blessed Father help me, I finally know what the key is . . . It is . . . oh the key.

The journal ended abruptly at this point, the last five or six pages left blank. A deep sadness filled Sally, mixed with a slow burning anger.

She knew as much as anyone knew about the Curse of the McCavendish family. She knew what happened on that fateful night when Matthew and his two associates went in search of the Gate, or she knew as much as Matthew cared to tell. She'd read how it led to his disgrace and downfall. She knew what he really conjured up in the woods—not a creature from Hell or from fairy land—and Sally knew that David and the rest of Matthew's family had been paying for it ever since.

Sally was reminded of the argument she'd had with her mother as a little girl when she'd quoted scripture. The sins of the father will be visited upon the child, she'd said, and her mother had vehemently disagreed. She would, Sally supposed. No parent wants to think of their children being punished for the mistakes they made.

Even still, if any proof were ever needed, it could be found in the crumbling brown pages of Matthew McCavendish's journal. His sins had been visited upon each generation of the McCavendish family for over two centuries and now they were being visited on David.

It all seemed so unfair. Was this really God's plan for her and David? Where was God in all of this? Was God a part of this in any way?

Sally had always wondered what it would be like to live in a world without God, if such a thing were even possible. Matthew had written of some strange heretical beliefs in his journal, of God being a prisoner in His own creation. If He really were experiencing Himself individually as every man woman and beast in creation, unaware of His divine totality, then it really wouldn't be possible to live in a world without God. Because not believing in God would mean not believing in the most vital part of yourself, the part that was God trapped in the material world. It would be like God not believing in Himself.

Sally wondered why she didn't take more comfort in this thought.

CHAPTER 20

SALLY WAS MORE certain now. Certain where she was going and certain she was doing the right thing.

This certainty didn't come from Hettie, Sally was sure of that. Hettie was nowhere to be seen or heard. This certainty came from her love for David. She'd gone to extraordinary lengths for him, but she was going to have him back. She was going to free him from the Beast. Sally had forsaken all her doubt. As strange as all this might seem, she knew why she was doing it.

She was deep in the forest where it was darker and cooler. The light was much dimmer as Sally stepped out of the undergrowth and approached the stream. The stream would take her to the glade where she was ultimately going.

Sally lingered by the undergrowth for a moment. There was one little thing that was playing on her mind, something she had to clear up before she could go through with everything she and Hettie had planned.

She stopped and turned back to look at the thicket of shrub. The dense undergrowth seemed to sense her hesitation and, as if from a great distance, a sudden gust moved through it. It moaned as it got closer to

Sally, and the tiny branches of the thicket struck each other with an increasing rhythm until the two came together and a voice emerged.

Sally smiled as soon as she heard it. Her stomach relaxed. Like a junkie who hears a dealer approach, she thought. The thought struck her as very apposite. It was why she had to have one last chat with Hettie.

"Why do you hold back—hold back—hold back—little sister?"

"There's something I need to know."

"Have we not taught you—taught you—taught you well?"

"You've taught me a lot of things, and there's certain things you wanted me to learn myself. That's why you told me about the journals, wasn't it?"

"Yes it was—it was—it was."

"It was something I read there that got me thinking. Every time you're around, every time I speak to you, my sadness, my anger, my doubt, it kind of trails off, disappears even."

"And why do you think—do you think—do you think that is?"

"I think you're taking it away from me. In the journal, Matthew McCavendish talked about beings who fed off bad emotions. He called them Bréost . . . wylmas, did I pronounce that right?"

"Close enough—enough—enough."

"That's what he was summoning in the glade. That's what came and took his soul. He never expected it to come as the Beast, but I don't think the Beast is the only thing that came through. I think something else snuck past him without him knowing—more Bréostwylmas. That's you isn't it?"

"You have learned well—learned well—learned well."

"Thank you. What I haven't worked out though, is why you hate the Beast so much if you're Bréostwylmas, too?"

"The Beast has committed a crime—a crime—a crime against us—against us—against us all. The worst type of crime—type of crime—type of crime for our kind."

"So it's like some sort of criminal in your world, and it escaped justice when Matthew opened a portal and summoned it. But you followed it here. McCavendish didn't realise he'd summoned you, too."

The thicket remained still. No voice came from it. Hettie's silence confirmed all of Sally's suspicions. She had one more question, though.

"Why wait until now to try and stop it? Why bide your time for over two centuries?"

"Because the time is right—is right—is right for the Gate to open."

The bodiless breeze left the thicket with an audible wheeze, like a dying breath escaping the lips of a corpse. Sally was all alone but purged of any bad feelings, as though she'd just had a good cry and gotten it all out of her system.

So that was why Hettie wanted her to read the journals, so she'd learn all about the Gate, the one that Matthew and his hapless colleagues encountered. Hettie had answered everything Sally had asked, but, as ever, she was only left with more questions. What was the Beast doing with David and his ancestors—collecting their souls in order to open the Gate? Was there a special number of souls it had to collect, or did they reach critical mass at some point and force the Gate open?

Maybe it had something to do with the right conjunction of stars or something like that. Whatever it was, it was pretty evident to Sally that David played a key part in it and that she was going to put a stop to it.

Matthew had written about the dangers of opening the Gate. It seemed to be the one thing he feared most. It seemed to be the one fear that lay behind everything everyone did in Dunballan, from the townsfolk to David himself, though no-one seemed to know what would happen if the Gate did open.

Sally wasn't about to let that happen, though. Tonight she was going to put a stop to it once and for all, and she had an otherworldly ally to help her.

CHAPTER 21

SALLY SMELLED THE glade before she actually stepped into it. Its scents were lush, primal, and sharp. There were deep mossy undertones, like the bark of the seven ancient elm trees whose thick trunks encircled the glade. There were high fragrant notes, like the pollen and the wild flowers that grew all across the clearing. There were plants here that had flourished for millennia, plants that couldn't be found anywhere else on the planet.

Sally couldn't help but catch her breath when she entered. The rest of the forest was often noisy, filled with a plethora of sounds. There were the raucous bird calls, the grunts and howls of the creatures that fought and foraged on the forest floor. There was the sound of the wind in the branches and the occasional rain on the leaves, and there were the thousand other unexplained noises that haunt such a wild and untamed territory.

The glade was a different matter altogether. There was hardly any noise here at all. It was as if all sound had been chased away by the seven huge elms and the other mystic forces that stood guard over it. Sally hardly dared to breathe here. She walked with as light a tread as possible, for fear of snapping a twig underfoot and disturbing the stillness. The silence only added to the sense of reverence that permeated the whole glade. It was a sign that it was one of the most sacred grounds on the planet. This was a Quiet Place.

Sally opened the Tupperware box as the moon rose above the glade and lit the whole area. It was a clear night, the moon was full and there were many stars overhead. The smells from the Tupperware box were quite different to anything else in the glade. The scent of the raw meat was really strong, as was the blood that leaked from it. They could not mask the aromas given off by the crushed leaves and berries with which it was seasoned though, nor the urine or semen in which it had been marinated.

These last two had been collected from David yesterday, after Sally had taken him to the glade. It hadn't been easy to get him there. He was as acquiescent as he always was when his soul was off with the Beast, but leading his empty, stumbling body through the forest's difficult terrain had been quite a hardship.

When Sally had finally gotten David to the glade, she had taken off his clothes and tied him to one of the elm trees. Then she'd shaved his head, his legs, his chest and his pubic regions, collecting all the hair in the wooden box to make into the figurine later. After that, Sally collected the fluids she needed from David, feeling completely disconnected from reality the whole time, unable to believe she was actually doing what she was doing. Hettie had said they needed the semen and urine to give the meat his scent so it would fool the Beast.

Sally had wanted to untie David and take him

home with her, but Hettie had cautioned against it. It was with great reluctance that she had left him naked and spread eagled against the tree, his wrists and ankles held by rope. She put the Tupperware box down and went over to him, running a hand across his bare scalp and cheek, his raw, shaven flesh puckered into little goose bumps.

His skin was pale and cold to the touch, his eyes were glazed, and he was breathing heavily through his mouth, but he didn't seem that worse for wear. It had been a mild, dry night and the glade was very sheltered from the wind. She had fretted about David as she walked all the way back from the forest in the dark. There was so much to prepare when she got back that strangely she had hardly given him a thought since. Looking at David now, Sally felt guilty about this, and she said a silent prayer that their scheme to thwart the Beast would work.

Sally left David and picked up the Tupperware box. She walked to the north entrance of the glade, between two of the largest elm trees, and began to lay a trail of steak chunks out into the forest to entice the Beast into the clearing. Her fingers soon became sticky with David's fluids.

When she'd used up all the meat, Sally came back into the glade and began to build a fire. She piled up kindling, fire-lighters and the volumes of Matthew's journal that she'd brought. She poured the paraffin she brought over the journals, so they'd burn better. Then she fetched the elm logs from the pile she'd collected earlier. She laid the logs around the paraffin soaked journals, the smallest in the centre, the largest around the outside, till finally she had a good sized bonfire.

Next, Sally fetched the two-kilogram bag of salt she'd brought, opened the bag and poured the salt on the ground near the bonfire, making a perfect circle all the way around it. Sally fetched the Zippo and the wooden box with the figurine she'd woven from all David's hair, and then she checked her watch. It was five minutes to midnight. She'd timed everything perfectly.

Sally lit the Zippo and threw it into the centre of the bonfire. The journals caught light straight away, and soon all of the logs were crackling with flames. The heat quickly became intense. Sally walked away from the flames until her toes were just inside the salt circle and her back was to the fire. She looked out at the north entrance, where the trail of meat led out into the forest, and she began to undress, folding all her clothes into a neat little pile beside her.

When she was totally naked, Sally began to chant in the loudest voice she could muster. Hettie had taught her the chant—it was in Anglo Saxon, the last language spoken by the followers of Matthew's strange heresy:

"Under fot wolues, under ueþer earnes,
under earnes clea, a þu geweornie.
Clinge þu alswa col on heorþe,
scring þu alswa scerne awage,
and weorne alswa weter on anbre."

As she was chanting, Sally heard movement and commotion in the forest just outside the glade. It was working, it was really working. She was summoning the Beast, drawing it into her trap. But the noises weren't coming from the north entrance, where she'd laid the meat. They were coming from a different part of the forest entirely.

By the light of the flames, Sally saw a woman in a bright orange waterproof stumble into the clearing. The woman blinked in the sudden glare of the flames. She was carrying a pocket torch that she shone first at Sally, making Sally shield her eyes, then at David. With the torchlight out of her eyes, Sally recognised the woman instantly, and she couldn't have been crosser about who it was.

"Jane, what the hell are you doing here?"

"Sally, oh God, it's worse than I thought. Stop. You have to stop this."

Even in the cold night air, Sally felt herself flush. Jane was the very last person Sally would want to see her naked. How dare she blunder into the glade while Sally had her unshaven legs and her cellulite on show? This was a private moment, it wasn't for Jane's or anybody else's eyes.

Sally covered her breasts with one arm and shooed Jane with the other.

"Get out of here, Jane. Get out of here now. You're going to ruin everything."

"Sally, listen to me, please listen to me. You can't do this. You don't understand."

"No, Jane, you don't understand, there's so much here that you don't know about."

"But you don't realise how many people you're going to hurt if you do this."

"Again, Jane, it's you who don't realise how many people I'm going to save."

"But you're not going save them like this. You don't realise what's at stake."

"And you do?"

"I saw first-hand, as a little girl, what can happen when we don't have a McCavendish in Dunballan. My Great Aunt was a little girl when Hamish McCavendish refused to come back here to live. She was the youngest to be affected at only five. The townsfolk let all the others die, but my Great Grandmother wouldn't let her go, and when she died, my mother and her brothers looked after her. She was the most hideous and pathetic thing you could ever see. She was an empty body, without any mind or soul. That shouldn't happen to any human being ever. That's why you have to stop this."

"Shut up, Jane, for once will you just shut up! You can't be here at this moment. You have to go, or I'll never get David back. I'll lose him forever."

"You won't lose him, that's the thing, he'll always come back to you. I know you hate what's happening to him, but at least he does come back to you. The rest of us aren't that lucky. That's why we need David, why we need both of you. Without David, we'd start to go, one by one, until there was no-one left in Dunballan with a soul and, unlike David, we don't get to come back. That's why I reached out to you, why I gave you the pamphlet, so you'd understand why David is so important, why we're all so grateful to you both. You don't know how much I risked in doing that. I was trying to be your friend."

"I don't want you as a friend!" Sally shouted. There, she'd finally said it to Jane's stupid, simpering face. She was glad it was out in the open. Maybe now Jane would leave her in privacy to finish the ritual.

If Jane spoiled everything by being here, if she kept

the Beast away or jeopardised the ritual, then Sally would pick up one of the logs from the fire and beat her skull in with it.

Before she had a chance to do that, there was movement on the outskirts of the glade. A huge, black form made its way into the clearing, raised its head, as if scenting the air, and then bowed it, as if in sorrow.

Jane shone her torch at the Beast. Neither its pelt nor its eyes reflected any of the torchlight. Instead the light seemed to fall into its form making it appear more of a shadow. A living moving shadow, the size of a small horse.

Jane screamed and dropped the torch. It shattered on the ground and went out. In the shimmering light of the fire, Jane started to back very slowly away from the Beast, moving towards the forest. She was making strange whimpering sounds in the back of her throat, and her face was bathed with sweat.

The Beast padded up to the very edge of the salt circle and stopped. It couldn't cross the circle which was enchanted, just like the meat it had eaten. Sally could see the meat had made it groggy. The Beast stood still, its head lowered, swaying ever so slightly on its paws.

This was Sally's chance, she had to strike now, while the Beast was incapacitated. She knelt, opened the wooden box and took out the figurine that she'd woven from David's hair. She held it up for the groggy creature to see. It was a replica of the Beast itself.

Now that she could compare her handiwork to the actual subject, Sally silently commended herself on the likeness. The Beast simply gazed at the woven figure with sadness and apprehension.

"Sally, please, for the last time," Jane called out. She was quite far away from the fire now, much closer to the trees. "Please don't do this."

"I thought I told you to shut up, Jane," Sally said.

"You and David aren't the only ones affected by this curse."

Sally ignored her. She was staring into the eyes of the Beast, and both of them were waiting to see what Sally would do next.

"All of us are affected," Jane said. "All the townsfolk, we're not allowed to leave and neither are our descendants. Anyone who's born here, anyone who settles here has been trapped since Matthew McCavendish summoned that Beast. That's why we're so cut off."

"And I'm about to free you," said Sally and began to chant again.

"Swa litel þu gewurþe alswa linsetcorn,
and miccli lesse alswa anes handwurmes hupeban,
And alswa litel þu gewurþe þet þu nawiht gewurþe."

Without taking her eyes off the Beast, Sally flung the woven figurine over her left shoulder and into the fire behind her.

"NO!" Jane shrieked.

Sally heard the figurine crackle and singe as the flames found it. A feeling of intense dread seized her, her stomach lurched, and it seemed as if the bottom had just dropped out of her world. She was suddenly on the verge of tears and hysteria.

Sally didn't know why, but she instantly regretted what she'd just done. She'd spent so long planning this, she'd prepared everything so carefully, but now it was done. In fact, the very second it was done, she knew intrinsically that something was very, very wrong.

The Beast arched its back, threw its head in the air, and roared with pain. David's body twitched and writhed as he fought his bonds, his muscles twisting and convulsing. His mouth began to froth, and then he too let out a long, pain filled scream.

Sally had torn him free of the Beast, plucked him from its breast with such finality, he could never return. Yet she felt no triumph in this, only a terrible and irrevocable doubt.

The Beast pressed itself up as close to the edge of the salt circle as it could get. It fixed Sally with its deep black eyes, as if to remonstrate with her. Sally could not look away. The eyes seemed to grow larger and larger until they filled her field of vision. The Beast seemed to reach out and build a bridge between their minds, and across this bridge it sent an unconscionable truth.

Sally saw, finally, all that had occurred on that fateful night when McCavendish had summoned the Bréostwylmas. She saw what actually came through from that higher realm, and she began to weep. Finally she had all the answers she sought, answers that didn't throw up further questions, answers that showed her the truth. A truth that crushed her spirit in the light of what she had just done.

David came back to himself, the light returned to his eyes and he looked about with confusion. He saw the ropes that held his wrists and ankles, he glanced at the fire and the Beast in panic. Sally tried to go to him, but she couldn't leave the circle. It was as though there was an invisible barrier inside the salt circle that pushed her back or simply stopped her every time she tried to leave.

She called out to David, begging him to talk to her, to tell her he was okay, but when he did, she wished more than anything that he hadn't. David's final words broke Sally completely, and she fell to the ground sobbing with an endless regret.

She was vaguely aware of Jane, some way off in the glade, wailing and crying herself. Sally looked up and searched her out in the waning firelight. Jane was on her knees, her hands clasped in prayer and her lips moving furiously. The words offered little consolation. She was shaking uncontrollably with fear.

The Beast began to twitch and shudder, its whole body seized by violent tremors. Its legs kept kicking out from under it, shaking violently as if it was trying to shake something off. The kicking and the shaking got worse, and the Beast started to gnaw at its limbs in fear and confusion.

The Beast howled in pain as its limbs began to bend back on themselves at impossible angles. Sally could hear joints pop, sinews snap, and bones crack. She had hated this creature, but now she could have cried, it was such a pitiable sight.

It didn't stop with the Beast's legs—soon its whole body began to fold in on itself, creasing and bending along dimensional angles that should not be possible on this plane of existence. The Beast's head thrashed around the whole time, its eyes filled with terror at what was happening to it.

Sally's eyes could not process what they were

seeing. The more she looked, the less she could work out what was happening, and it hurt her brain to try. All she could tell for sure was that the Beast was being pulled into itself and was tearing the air around it.

Only it wasn't quite the air it was tearing, it was the space, too. This was a Quiet Place, a place of immense and terrible power, and something was happening here that shouldn't happen anywhere, not in this world or any others.

A huge rent was appearing in the place where the Beast had been—it looked like a tear in a theatre backdrop, only this tear was in the fabric of existence itself. It grew into a giant rent that was almost impossible to look at. It was unnatural, inverting every law of time and space that Sally knew about.

Like a black hole, it was bending the space around it. The rent seemed to have its own gravity, drawing things to it with an inescapable force. The rent was pulling souls and other incorporeal beings to it, with a power that could not be denied. Sally felt the tug herself, felt her primal essence leap, with a longing to leave, deep inside. Only the salt circle kept her safe.

A thick black mist, full of sharp mouths and inky tendrils leapt out of the undergrowth and spiralled into the rent, then disappeared. Sally realised that this was Hettie in her true form, going back to her natural habitat. Seeing Hettie in this light, Sally was riven with betrayal, but she was also aware of her own complicity in this deception.

Hettie had never once lied to her. She was simply judicious with the truth, and she had even warned Sally of what would happen, but, as with every story she'd read of Hettie in the pamphlet, Sally had not heeded, or understood, the warning. She had chosen to interpret everything Hettie told her according to her own needs. Hettie's motives might have been malign, but Sally had manipulated herself. She also saw that Jane too, in trying to reach out to Sally, had failed to heed Hettie's warning to the townsfolk.

Jane screamed, and Sally tore her eyes away from the rent to look at her, on the edge of the glade. The scream was a pitiable, heart wrenching sound. It was as much a cry of protest at the unfairness and inhumanity of the situation, as it was a cry of fear and pain.

Sally watched as the most essential part of Jane, the one thing that made her most human, was torn from her body. It didn't go freely, as David's had when it entered the Beast. It was dragged, unwillingly from her and pulled into the rent, the rift in space where the Beast had once stood. One minute she was Jane, begging God not to let this happen, the next she was a mindless, soulless husk.

David's soul went next, leaving his body like the dying prayer of a murder victim. Then it was Sally's turn to scream and protest. She tried to run to him, to hold him, to stop it from happening, but the barrier of the salt circle kept her where she was, no matter how many times she flung herself against it.

Then came the souls of every living being in the forest, followed by those of the townsfolk of Dunballan. Sally only saw them as they entered the rift, they were invisible to her until then. But even if she couldn't see them, she could sense every one.

As they came faster and with more frequency, it was like being at the centre of a howling maelstrom.

The most vital, divine and immortal component of so many human beings shrieked past her, wrenched from their owners' bodies.

Sally felt the fear, and the longing for more life, emanating from them. Felt the injustice that so many hopes and aspirations had been crushed. So much vibrancy, nobility and the better part of their humanity was now laid to waste. It came from them all, every adult and child, like a high pitched frequency that resonated in the depths of Sally's own soul.

The Gate had opened. Matthew McCavendish's greatest fear had come to pass. The Gate had opened between this world and the worlds beyond, the worlds he had written of in his journal. The Gate was supposed to free the souls that passed through it from the prison of Creation. That's what Matthew had written in his journal. But the Gate wasn't opening in the worlds beyond, it was opening in this one, and the souls that passed through it had to run a very deadly gauntlet first.

Sally watched, entranced as the rift was pushed wider and wider by the volume of souls passing through it. She witnessed the entities that bore down on the newly harvested souls, as if they were descending on a banquet. They seemed to be made of impossible shapes, formed by some unknown geometry that constantly reformed itself into curves and angles that should never have existed.

These must be the Archons. They were far worse than Matthew had described. He'd called them guardians of the furthest limits of creation, but something had gone horribly wrong. They weren't stopping the souls from leaving Creation, they were devouring, desecrating and despoiling them.

Starved of sustenance for so long, the Archons were brutal and gluttonous in their feeding. They were surrounded by a thick black cloud of Bréostwylmas. Sally saw them swarm round the Archons with their famished mouths outstretched, drinking in the suffering and the agony of their victims.

Sally screamed at them, begged for them to show a little mercy. She beat her fists against the invisible barrier that left her impotent. Neither the souls, the Archons, nor the Bréostwylmas paid Sally's pleas the slightest attention. They were in a different realm of existence.

Long eternities later, when Sally's mind had become numb to the atrocities she'd witnessed, when the last embers of the fire had fallen to ash and the sun had begun to creep into the sky, the Gate swung shut. The rift between the world closed up and silence fell once again on the glade.

Sally picked herself up off the ground with shaking, frozen limbs, and found her clothes. Her throat was hoarse from screaming, her joints were sore and swollen, and her chest rattled from the long hours she'd spent naked in the cold night air.

She kicked the salt into the ashes of the fire, put everything away in her big cloth bag, then went and dressed David. She took David and Jane's bodies by the hand and led them out of the wood and down the hill to Dunballan.

The silence that had once filled the glade now reigned over the forest and the town.

EPILOGUE

RIGHT NOW:

SALLY STOOD AT the sink, staring at the butcher, with a cup of water in her hands. She was frozen into inaction by the sheer weight of her memories and tiredness. She didn't have the energy to move.

She knew she should bring the water to the boy on the sofa, maybe find more blankets and some paracetamol for his fever. He would die soon, like his mother, if she didn't help him, but then so would most of the townsfolk.

Sally was exhausted. She had been worn out just looking after David, but now she had a whole town to look after. More than two thousand people, all of them in the same state as David. She fretted constantly about David—she had to leave him alone for considerable lengths of time, and she worried about his safety. She felt guilty for abandoning him so much, but she couldn't abandon everyone else in Dunballan either, not after what she'd done to them.

Sometimes Sally fantasised about having help, a friend to share her duties or even a small group of volunteers. Occasionally her fantasies would involve one of the townsfolk suddenly waking and coming back to themselves, forgiving her for what she did, listening to her side of the story, and understanding her motives. Then they would join her in tending to the townsfolk, organising schemes and systems that would help her look after them en masse, in some large hall or something.

Ironically that person would often be Jane, whose friendship she had shunned, and whose advances Sally had rebuffed. More than anything now, she wanted Jane's forgiveness, her understanding, and yes, she wasn't ashamed to admit it, Jane's companionship. She wanted that almost as much as she wanted David back. Jane had been right, he had always come back to her before. He was never coming back now, nor was anyone else in Dunballan.

Her other fantasy involved a small group coming to Dunballan, either a hiking party who stayed to give her a hand when they grasped what was going on, or an outside rescue team or even a girl guide troop, she didn't mind. She would drill them all, and they would set about feeding, washing and cleaning up after all the townsfolk, so that their every need was met. They would do this without question, they would do it because it was the right thing to do, and they would never ask Sally how everyone had come to be the way they were.

Sally knew that no one was coming to help, or relieve her, though. Dunballan was very remote. It wasn't on any through roads, there was no rail connection, and no one made regular deliveries there. That's how the locals had always wanted it, and Sally now knew why that was.

It might be months, even years, before anyone stumbled on the little town, and by that point more than half of them would probably be dead, in spite of Sally's best efforts. Until then Sally would be forced to shoulder this whole burden herself. She would have to go on sleeping two or three hours a night and running herself ragged trying to keep as many of them as clean and as well fed as she could, while watching hundreds more of them simply die.

Sally had toyed with the idea of leaving Dunballan to go and get outside help, but she wasn't certain if the authorities could do anything to help. By the time she got them to listen to her, to mobilise the sort of help she'd need, most of the townsfolk would be dead anyway, and they'd never believe her if she told them how everyone came to be in the state they were in.

If she was honest though, she really didn't want anyone to help her. She felt too guilty, too responsible. This was Sally's problem, and it was down to Sally to fix it, whether it killed her or not.

Sally's reverie was broken by a sharp clatter. She looked up and saw that the Butcher, standing in front of the counter had opened his tightly clenched fist. When she saw what had fallen from it, Sally laughed a bitter laugh, her first in over a week. At the butcher's feet was a brass key.

It sat on the ancient linoleum like an accusation, a cruel reminder of what she'd hoped to do and how badly wrong it had all gone. The key was like an emblem of everything that had gone wrong. Sally realised that as soon as the Beast had fixed her with its baleful eyes.

She thought back to that moment now, while she'd stood with her back to the fire and listened to the flames consume the figurine of the Beast she'd made from David's hair. Standing at the very edge of the salt circle, the Beast had opened a bridge between their minds.

What it had sent across into Sally's mind was a lived experience, memories and emotions so intense they were burned into her consciousness with a clarity that none of her own memories could ever hope to match. Recalling them now, Sally found them just as vivid as when she had first experienced them.

To begin with, Sally had seen the Gate that Matthew had written about in his journal. She not only saw it, but she became aware that it was far more conscious and intelligent than Matthew had ever guessed. She was also aware of the deep and unfathomable sorrow that it felt.

Clustered around the gate, like packs of scavengers, were the Archons. Once they had served a higher purpose, maintaining the integrity of Creation, but now they had become corrupt and degraded. They had developed an appetite for the pious souls that were attracted to the Gate and the promise it offered of becoming one with God.

Instead of warning those souls away and keeping them within the material plane, the Archons had begun to prey on the souls and devour them, using the Gate as bait, to draw souls to them for sport. The pain and suffering this caused the Gate was beyond the capacity of any language to express. This was the very last thing that it wanted, but it was stuck fast in its position and could not leave. Or so the Archons believed.

It was the suffering of the Gate that first drew the Bréostwylmas to it. They bedded in and began to flourish on the extreme and lengthy suffering of the

Archons' victims. This state of affairs only hurt the Gate more, and this increase in the Gate's suffering drew more Bréostwylmas to it.

To the Gate, this whole situation was worse than intolerable, it was unconscionable. The Gate was fashioned from the deepest vein of God's mercy. It was meant as an escape and a release, not an instrument of torture, not a lure to feed the most merciless and draconian elements of Creation.

The Gate, however, had more patience, and more cunning, than either the Archons or the Bréostwylmas ever realised. So it bided its time, and it waited, knowing that a chance would come to be rid of its persecutors.

Then something happened that neither the Gate, the Archons, nor the Bréostwylmas ever expected— Matthew McCavendish opened a portal in a Quiet Place, one of the most powerful spaces on the earthly plane. Matthew had been to the Gate before, the Gate recognised him, and his energy was like a lightning rod to a thunderbolt. It gave the Gate impetus and direction, and it allowed it to tear up its roots and move from a higher plane to an earthly one.

Matthew was hoping to summon one of the Bréostwylmas, but he got far more than he bargained for. Before the Archons or the Bréostwylmas could do a thing, the Gate left its position and flew through the portal Matthew had opened.

The Gate found that it could not maintain its shape or form on a lower plane, though—it had to choose a new one. It also found that it could not keep itself closed for long periods without assistance, and this might prove disastrous.

That was when Sally realised she wasn't just

sharing the Beast's memories, she was also sharing the Gate's recollections. For the Beast and the Gate were one and the same.

Sally learned all this too late, and she wasn't certain she'd have acted differently if she'd already known. It was only David's last words to her, when she'd torn him from the Beast that caused her to bitterly regret her actions. When she learned what Matthew had meant in his final journal entry and what he'd bequeathed to his successors.

"No, Sally, no!" David had shrieked. "I'm the key! It's me, I'm what's keeping it shut!"

By then it was too late. The Gate had opened, and wherever it should have led, the Archons were waiting hungrily on the other side.

Sally had wanted to unlock David from the moment they first met. She was always afraid of the consequences, though. Hettie had even warned her against unlocking him but, like all Hettie's warnings, it had gone unheeded. Now she finally knew what those consequences were.

David's living soul, the part of him that was God, had been torn out and devoured, along with everything that was Divine in every living being in Dunballan.

Sally had always wondered what it would be like to live in a world without God, if such a thing were even possible.

At last, she had her answer. It was where she found herself right now, surrounded by the soulless shells for which she cared, out of a guilt she would never assuage, in a town that God would never know again.

It was where, she was quite certain, she would soon die and no-one would ever know what she had endured.

POOR SALLY, ONLY YOU, GENTLE READER, KNOW WHAT SHE ENDURED. SHE THOUGHT FREEING DAVID WAS THE KEY TO ALL THEIR PROBLEMS. THAT IT WOULD RELEASE THEM FROM THE BURDEN OF DUNBALLAN'S TOWN FOLK.
BUT DAVID WAS THE KEY TO RELEASING SOMETHING FAR WORSE. AND THE PEOPLE OF DUNBALLAN HAVE BECOME FAR MORE OF A BURDEN TO HER.
IF THIS STORY HAS UNLOCKED ANYTHING IN YOU, GENTLE READER, I HOPE IT'S A BURNING DESIRE TO READ MORE BOOKS IN THE BARK BITES HORROR SERIES. IN FACT, I PREDICT THAT WILL BE THE KEY TO YOUR FUTURE HAPPINESS.
POLIWKO

QUIET PLACES—THE SOUNDTRACK

A PLAYLIST

As I began writing the revised and expanded version of this novella, I discovered a group of musicians, artists and tricksters who were attempting, with their music, art, and online presence, to do what I was trying to do in my writing with *Quiet Places*. Bob Fischer's excellent article, "The Haunted Generation," in the June 2017 issue of Fortean Times, was my entry point and I soon became fascinated with their work. The work of these creators has been dubbed 'Hauntology' by the author and journalist Simon Reynolds, a term he borrowed from Jacques Derrida but repurposed in this instance.

As Reynolds defines it, in his sleeve notes to *In a Moment*—a compilation album put out by the label, Ghost Box—'Hauntology' involves any series of works that " . . . have filled me with mournful wonder at the thought of the country I'd grown up in, in the '60s and '70s, a country that has subsequently been very deliberately eroded away. A time/place where/when a young mind could access all kinds of cultural riches and frissons through the local library (and the inter-library loan system), through a public broadcasting culture that was dedicated to challenging viewers and listeners with unsettling children's programmes like *The Changes*, *The Children of The Stones*, and *The Clifton House Mystery*, peculiar plays *like Stargazy on Zummerdown*, radio phonic dramas and sounds capes like *Inferno Revisited* and *Inventions for Radio*."

I was a very young child in the '70s and early '80s, before the neo-liberal policies of Reagan and Thatcher began to re-shape western society, and it was a very strange time in which to grow up, especially in Britain. TV programmes like the aforementioned *Children of The Stones* were utterly terrifying, but not quite as terrifying as the Public Information Films regularly shown on TV, warning me not to play by dark and lonely waters or in electricity sub-stations. Children's fiction often had a weird hallucinogenic feel to it and it was easy to read your way through the entire children's section of the local library, and to progress to the inappropriate adult fiction, without anyone batting an eyelid. All of this helped shape my consciousness and I was delighted, when I discovered 'Hauntology' to find I wasn't the only one.

As much as Quiet Places is influenced by my love of Arthur Machen, Charlotte Gilman Perkins, Algernon Blackwood, and Clark Ashton Smith, it is also hugely influenced by the folk horror I watched on TV as a confused and terrified child in the '70s and early '80s, dramas such as *Penda's Fen*, *The Changes*, *The Stone Tape* and episodes of *Nigel Kneale's Beasts* like "During Barty's Party and Baby." I was trying to channel the fear and sense of unreality I felt, watching those programmes, through a contemporary lens, and to tap into an alternate history while I was doing so. Once again, to my great delight, I discovered a series of artists, on labels like Ghostbox and Clay Pipe who were doing just that in music.

The following playlist is drawn from the albums I listened to as I wrote this long novella. Their blend of folk and electronica is strange, slightly eerie and riven with nostalgia for a lost age that probably never existed, outside of the liminal spaces in the artist's memory. It's not meant to be listened to in any particular order, but I think any of these albums might enhance your appreciation of this book, unless you like to read in total silence. If you're at all curious, all the listed items are available on Amazon, iTunes, and a few can even be found on Bandcamp.

QUIET PLACES PLAYLIST:

Artist	Album	Label
The Advisory Circle	As the Crow Flies	Ghostbox
Belbury Poly	From an Ancient Star	Ghostbox
Jon Brooks	Shapwick	ClayPipe/Cafe Kaput
The Focus Group	Hey Let Loose Your Love	Ghostbox
Boards of Canada	Geogaddi	Beat Records
Belbury Poly	The Belbury Tales	Ghostbox
The Focus Group	Sketches and Spells	Ghostbox
The Advisory Circle	Other Channels	Ghostbox

ACKNOWLEDGEMENTS

Writing is a very solitary pursuit, but publishing a book is a group effort. Much as I would like to hog all the glory for myself, too many people know where too many bodies are buried, and some of them have drawn maps (damn them). So, to stop those maps ever making their way into the public domain, I am forced to 'fess up and thank all those people who have helped this book make its way to your hot, sticky hands.

A good editor is a Godsend to an author, and I had two on this book. The first was Steve J. Shaw, who originally commissioned this story for *Great British Horror 1—Green and Pleasant Land*. This long novella was supposed to be a short story of no longer than 7,000 words, however, like an irradiated amoeba on a mad scientist's Petri dish, the story kept growing and growing and just wouldn't stop. As the deadline loomed I contacted Steve to tell him of my dilemma and, like the true gentleman he is, he told me to keep working on it and he would hold the deadline for as long as he could. It was down to the wire though and I only just made it, adding at least 100 pages to the final anthology and taking up every seat on the back row, like an annoying customer on a Ryanair flight. Without Steve's unflagging support and encouragement, this story might never have seen the light of day and I am truly grateful for all his help and honored to have been in such an exceptional anthology.

Monique Snyman edited this book for Crystal Lake

Publishing not once, but twice. This is because I have the unfortunate habit of rewriting my manuscripts, often from scratch, after the first set of edits. In this instance I not only rewrote a good 5/6 of the original manuscript, I added another 12,000 words making it a third as long again. Monique took this all in her stride and was unbelievably gracious in the face of the total sanction I placed on semi-colons, a type of punctuation for which she has an especial fondness. She was meticulous in going over the text to improve it and caught several howling blunders that would have been very embarrassing to me if she hadn't. That she did all this with the greatest possible speed and efficiency is near to miraculous, both Crystal Lake and I are lucky to have her as an editor.

Head honcho Joe Mynhardt edited all my previous works for Crystal Lake, and did an amazing job on them. Over the past four years he has become a tireless promoter of my work, a constant collaborator and close personal friend. I think I'm still the only Crystal Lake author to have travelled all the way to Bloemfontein, with my family, to have dinner with Joe and his lovely wife Annemie.

Next I want to thank two reviewers, who didn't exactly give me a glowing write up when "Quiet Places" appeared in *Great British Horror 1* last year—Paul Michaels and Des Lewis. No one likes to get a mediocre review, and while it's not conventional to thank your critics, sometimes they really are doing you a favor. Paul and Des pointed out certain shortcomings in the original text and it is partly due to their reviews that I rewrote it again from scratch, forcing poor Monique to edit it all over again. I would like to think that thanks to Paul and Des' comments, and Monique's edits, this work is now much improved.

Many websites have been incredibly kind with their encouragement and support of my work over the past few years and I think it's only fair to thank Jim McCleod and Kit Power of Gingernuts of Horror, Michael Wilson and Bob Pastorella of This Is Horror, Tim Cundle and Jim Dodge of Mass Movement Magazine, Paula Limbaugh of Horror Novel Reviews, Angela Crawford at Horror Maiden's Book Reviews and Nev Murray and Chad Clark of Confessions of a Reviewer.

Many fellow writers and friends have been extremely supportive of me on social media and I'd like to extend a huge thanks to Ramsey Campbell and Stephen Volk, for giving me great quotes. Also Samantha Hill, Charlotte Munroe, Toneye Eyenot, Jaime Johnesee, David Dubrow, Rob Shepherd, Mark Leney, Dave Jeffrey, Theresa Derwin, Vix Kirkpatrick, The Slaughter Sisters, Jason Morton, Jason Kelly, Tina Marie, Mallory Haws, Marcie Fraser, Yvonne Davis, Zak A. Ferguson and Marianne Elise.

There are hundreds of other people who have helped me and I'm sure I've forgotten to mention too many of them here. If you're one of them please accept my apologies, remove the pins from that voodoo doll and drop me a line. I will apologize and include you in a set of future acknowledgements. I promise.

The End?

Not if you want to dive into more of Crystal Lake Publishing's Tales from the Darkest Depths!

Check out our amazing website and online store
or download our latest catalog here.
https://geni.us/CLPCatalog

Looking for award-winning Dark Fiction?
Download our latest catalog.

Includes our anthologies, novels, novellas, collections,
poetry, non-fiction, and specialty projects.

WHERE STORIES COME ALIVE!

We always have great new projects and content on the website to dive into, as well as a newsletter, behind the scenes options, social media platforms, our own dark fiction shared-world series and our very own webstore. Our webstore even has categories specifically for KU books, non-fiction, anthologies, and of course more novels and novellas.

ABOUT THE AUTHOR

Multiple award-winning author, Jasper Bark is infectious—and there's no known cure. If you're reading this you're already contaminated. The symptoms will manifest any time soon. There's nothing you can do about it. There's no itching or unfortunate rashes, but you'll become obsessed with his mind-bending books.

Then you'll want to tell everyone else about his visionary horror fiction. About its originality, its wild imagination and how it takes you to the edge of your sanity. We're afraid there's no way to avoid this. These words contain a power you're hopeless to resist. You're already in their thrall, you know you are. You're itching to read all of Jasper's bloodstained books. Don't fight this urge, embrace it. You've been bitten by the Bark bug and you love it!

Would you like to read five more of Jasper's books absolutely free?

Of course you would. I mean, who doesn't like free books?

Jasper's infamous novella, *Stuck On You* is now free to own as soon as you join Jasper's cult and sign up to his mailing list through the QR code below.

Don't worry, you won't have to shave your head or unalive any celebrities (for the first couple of years). But you will get all of Jasper's latest, videos, podcasts, blogs, breaking news on upcoming books and other crucial information to help you cyberstalk him.

What's more, you'll get two more short novels, a graphic novel and a spoof picture book, just to sweeten the deal! That's five free books just for signing up. These books are exclusive to this offer. You won't get them anywhere else.

Are we crazy? Of course we're crazy! We're asking you to join Jasper's cult!
And because we know you can't bear to miss out.

Don't be the only weird kid on your block to miss out. Don't delay. Sign up today.

Readers . . .

Thank you for reading *Quiet Places*. We hope you enjoyed this novel. If you have a moment, please review *Quiet Places* at the store where you bought it.

Help other readers by telling them why you enjoyed this book. No need to write an in-depth discussion. Even a single sentence will be greatly appreciated. Reviews go a long way to helping a book sell, and is great for an author's career. It'll also help us to continue publishing quality books.

Thank you again for taking the time to journey with Crystal Lake Publishing.

You will find links to all our social media platforms on our Linktree page.
https://linktr.ee/CrystalLakePublishing

MISSION STATEMENT

Since its founding in August 2012, Crystal Lake Publishing has quickly become one of the world's leading publishers of Dark Fiction and Horror books. In 2023, Crystal Lake Publishing formed a part of Crystal Lake Entertainment, joining several other divisions, including Torrid Waters, Crystal Lake Comics, Crystal Lake Kids, and many more.

While we strive to present only the highest quality fiction and entertainment, we also endeavour to support authors along their writing journey. We offer our time and experience in non-fiction projects, as well as author mentoring and services, at competitive prices.

With several Bram Stoker Award wins and many other wins and nominations (including the HWA's Specialty Press Award), Crystal Lake Publishing puts integrity, honor, and respect at the forefront of our publishing operations.

We strive for each book and outreach program we spearhead to not only entertain and touch or comment on issues that affect our readers, but also to strengthen and support the Dark Fiction field and its authors.

Not only do we find and publish authors we believe are destined for greatness, but we strive to work with men and women who endeavour to be decent human beings who care more for others than themselves, while still being hard working, driven, and passionate artists and storytellers.

Crystal Lake Publishing is and will always be a beacon of what passion and dedication, combined with overwhelming teamwork and respect, can accomplish. We endeavour to know each and every one of our readers, while building personal relationships with our authors, reviewers, bloggers, podcasters, bookstores, and libraries.

We will be as trustworthy, forthright, and transparent as any business can be, while also keeping most of the headaches away from our authors, since it's our job to solve the problems so they can stay in a creative mind. Which of course also means paying our authors.

We do not just publish books, we present to you worlds within your world, doors within your mind, from talented authors who sacrifice so much for a moment of your time.

There are some amazing small presses out there, and through collaboration and open forums we will continue to support other presses in the goal of helping authors and showing the world what quality small presses are capable of accomplishing. No one wins when a small press goes down, so we will always be there to support hardworking, legitimate presses and their authors. We don't see Crystal Lake as the best press out there, but we will always strive to be the best, strive to be the most interactive and grateful, and even blessed press around. No matter what happens over time, we will also take our mission very seriously while appreciating where we are and enjoying the journey.

What do we offer our authors that they can't do for themselves through self-publishing?

We are big supporters of self-publishing (especially hybrid publishing), if done with care, patience, and planning. However, not every author has the time or inclination to do market research, advertise, and set up book launch strategies. Although a lot of authors are successful in doing it all, strong small presses will always be there for the authors who just want to do what they do best: write.

What we offer is experience, industry knowledge, contacts and trust built up over years. And due to our strong brand and trusting fanbase, every Crystal Lake Publishing book comes with weight of respect. In time our fans begin to trust our judgment and will try a new author purely based on our support of said author.

With each launch we strive to fine-tune our approach, learn from our mistakes, and increase our reach. We continue to assure our authors that we're here for them and that we'll carry the weight of the launch and dealing with third parties while they focus on their strengths—be it writing, interviews, blogs, signings, etc.

We also offer several mentoring packages to authors that include knowledge and skills they can use in both traditional and self-publishing endeavours.

We look forward to launching many new careers.

This is what we believe in. What we stand for. This will be our legacy.

**Welcome to Crystal Lake Publishing—
Tales from the Darkest Depths.**

* 9 7 8 1 6 4 0 0 7 4 7 0 5 *